"Remember when you first read the stories of Clive Barker, or T.E.D. Klein, or Thomas Ligotti, or John Shirley, or Dennis Etchison, or David J. Schow, or Lucy Taylor, or Caitlin Keirnan, or Michael Shea, or Melanie Tem, and realized you were in the presence of a major talent in modern horror? I got the same feeling reading Nicolay. He steers clear of stock monsters and tropes of the horror genre. His fiction is clear-sighted, hard-edged, realistic, Raymond Carver-like. . ." —*Dead Reckonings*

"Nicolay's punch is grim and honest, his horizons vast, alluring, and keenly attuned to what unfurls in our darkest dreams."
—Joseph S. Pulver, Sr, author of *Blood Will Have Its Season*

"Nicolay lays claim to the attention of everyone interested in the future of weird fiction, and his claim is a strong one indeed."
—John Langan, author of *The Wide Carnivorous Sky and Other Monstrous Geographies*

"Scott Nicolay is consistently one of the most exciting and original voices in modern weird fiction. His prose is exquisite, inventive, savage, and chilling, without being beholden to pulp-era titans. This is Weird Literature, circa now."
—Ross E. Lockhart, editor of *Cthulhu Fhtagn!* and *The Children of Old Leech*

"We are not in the presence of a callow and bullish youth, but a man of erudition and experience. Nicolay is one who has seen much, endured much, has undergone prolonged pressure and the result is a diamond among stones."
—Laird Barron, author of *The Beautiful Thing That Awaits Us All*


"Nicolay's writing is clean-limbed, not a shred of rococco excess on it. Poetry and the demotic mix well in his prose. He expertly delivers clues and foreshadowings and backstory tidbits attendant upon his enigmas and frights without hammering the reader over the head with gore or hyperbole. His characters are engrossing, if often repellant, his plotting assured, and his venues enticingly nasty." —*Locus*


"Scott Nicolay is a writer in the tradition of modern practitioners of the weird such as Mark Samuels, Terry Lamsley, and Laird Barron. He gives us the unease of Ligotti with the fluid prose of Clark Ashton Smith. *Ana Kai Tangata* is a serious contender for best collection of the year." —*This Is Horror*


"The first thing that hits you while reading Scott Nicolay. . . That old black magic that comes with encountering great weird fiction for the first time." —*Crows N' Bones*

# *Noctuidae*

## SCOTT NICOLAY

A KING SHOT BOOK
Portland | Athens

FIRST KING SHOT PRESS EDITION

King Shot Press
P.O. Box 80601
Portland, OR 97280

Copyright © 2016 by Scott Nicolay

Cover design copyright © 2016 Matthew Revert
www.matthewrevert.com

Interior design by Michael Kazepis

All rights reserved. No part of this book may be reproduced or transmitted in any form or by any means, electronic or mechanical, including photocopying, recording, or by any information storage and retrieval system, without the written consent of the publisher, except where permitted by law.

This is a work of fiction. All names, characters, places, and incidents are the product of the author's imagination. Where the names of actual celebrities or corporate entities appear, they are used for fictional purposes and do not constitute assertions of fact. Any resemblance to real events or persons, living or dead, is coincidental.

ISBN 978-0-9972518-1-4
Printed in the United States of America

Scott Nicolay was born in New Jersey but now lives in the desert where he keeps a garden and a rather large library. As a teacher, he and his students co-founded the New Mexico Youth Poetry Slam and the National Youth Poetry Slam. *Ana Kai Tangata*, his first book of weird horror tales, was published by Fedogan & Bremer in 2014. His story "Do You Like To Look at Monsters?" won the 2015 World Fantasy Award for Best Short Fiction, and "Eyes Exchange Bank" was selected for the inaugural (2014) edition of *The Year's Best Weird Fiction*. He hosts "The Outer Dark," a weekly podcast on Project iRadio featuring interviews with writers and artists in the ongoing Weird Renaissance. His second collection, *And at My Back I Always Hear*, approaches completion. For more information, visit www.scottnicolay.com.

**Also by Scott Nicolay**

*Ana Kai Tangata*
*The Bad Outer Space*
*Do You Like to Look At Monsters?*
*after*
*The Croaker*

*For the stolen children*

# *Noctuidae*

. . . it's easy enough to think of most of us as deep-sea fishes of a kind.

CHARLES FORT

The river flowed right over the road in places but they crossed it barely slowing. A trickle only a few inches deep right now, Sue-Min knew it meant the folks who lived in this canyon were stuck here during floods, maybe months at a time.

They probably didn't mind.

If you lived here of your own free will, you had to be happy here. You probably weren't that interested in human company, at least not from outside. You probably had supplies laid in to last a while. And a generator.

She could see the appeal. Deep in and well down Forest Road 281, the Blue River Canyon opened eventually into a narrow valley, widest on the west side of the river, such as it was. There the view stretched to near green hills rising right to green mountains, behind these a higher rolling row of purple mountains—*majesties!*—her backbrain sung the full phrase on its own, fragment from her earliest encounters with English—and beyond and above these a line of blue-gray peaks higher still in the haze, the sort of range one might mistake for clouds in the twilight, if the twilight were the sort in which one might also mistake clouds for mountains.

Sue-Min let her head slump back against the weathered seatback's cracked black leather, willing to let the scenery settle her edginess. It really was a damn fine day, despite her half hangover and shitty mood. As much of the sky as she could see overhead was unbroken turquoise. Maybe their day, their hike, would go okay despite it all.

So far, nothing went the way they planned on this trip. First Pete's date cancelled and left them three instead of four. Sue-Min tried to hint to Ron her discomfort with this configuration but he remained oblivious. What could she do? If Ron went, she was going too.

Then the ranchers.

What their topo map failed to show them was how 281, the only road down the Blue River, led straight onto a private ranch, ended there in fact, wide open cattle gate but handpainted NO TRESPASSING signs nailed to the grooved and massive cottonwood trunk beside it. Red paint. Their intended trailhead into Forest Service land and the Middle Blue lay somewhere beyond this private holding.

Though Pete never slowed as he passed the signs, Sue-Min saw them clearly on her side despite the overhanging foliage and shade. She drew in breath to call attention to the warnings, then exhaled. Pete must know what he was doing. Perhaps he met with the landowners in advance, squared things away. She hadn't paid much attention when he and Ron were planning—as a rule, she avoided Pete as much as possible—though she had to admit she was curious to meet his date for this backpacking trip, wanted to see what kind of girl would agree to a remote overnight hike with such a creeper. Only she wouldn't meet the mystery date, not this time. Easy to see why she cancelled—if she ever existed in the first place.

Pete drove on past a squat weathered ranch house, torn orange gingham curtains hanging askew in the windows, fabric likely once red now paled from long sun. They passed low tilting water tanks and clumps of rusted farm machinery hedged in by bleached tufts of high dead brush. Scattered grazing cattle. A mile or so beyond the gate and signs the road petered out, their rough rutted route concluding in a diminished riverbed choked with weeds and cobbles. To their left extended a turnout of sorts, dirt banked in berms ahead of room for several vehicles, marks of steel tread and claws still visible on the soil. Someone had an earth mover, although she hadn't seen it while passing the ranch. Pete braked the truck just shy of the furthest berm and they all three climbed out to stretch and gear up.

Not two minutes and a pair of 4 wheel ATVs buzzed up behind their truck. Right before Sue-Min heard them approach she'd been eyeing some bushes where she thought she could squat in privacy. Too late.

The riders were weather-beaten white men, both in Resistol hats, cotton shirts tucked tight into Wranglers. One was stocky and graying, the other lanky and leathered though likely less than thirty. The rancher and his son or hired hand. She guessed the latter based on their lack of physical resemblance. Both rode with shotguns on their ATVs in plastic scabbards like tubes for rural newspaper delivery, and as they slid from their seats both drew those weapons. Drew, but did not raise or level them. The two men let their guns hang at six, seven o'clock. The level of threat was implicit but limited, deferred.

She caught the hand's eyes flicking on and off her, up and down, that blend of lust and slow rage she knew too well from elsewhere. Smoldering anger over her apparent foreignness, at the shape of her eyes, at her presence in their stronghold. For once she was glad of the Glock Ron kept in his pack, preferred not to think how Pete probably packed one too. Pete was the kind of guy saw unpermitted concealed carry as a point of pride, a civic duty.

Ron found Sue-Min's hand with his, held it, squeezed. Pete strode ahead to wade in, asking, —Hey guys, have we got a prob—? but Ron called him back, took the lead. He released Sue-Min's hand, strolled out to the pair and spoke. The wind struck up in the leaves overhead so she and Pete heard little more than the general rhythm of the conversation, its ebb and flow. They watched the mismatched sides commence a session of head shaking, hand pointing, the odd nod here and there. At least the two men never brought their guns to bear.

That would've meant *time to go* . . . unless it meant *too late to go*. How close did things come to going that far south? She wasn't sure she wanted to know. Pete sidled toward Sue but she stepped away, determined not to bond.

She had confidence in Ron. She'd watched him work his magic before with surly ranchers on caving trips in the GypKap. Gotten them access to sites no one had seen in a generation or more. His first ten years raised just outside Carrizozo had left him with some social skills in southern NM and AZ, the rural version of street smarts. Pete probably would've got them shot.

Several minutes into the conversation the younger rancher pointed back the way they'd come then over the ridge to his right, their left. After final nods and even a lifeless half smile by the senior rancher, a flat expression that never reached his eyes, all parties retreated to their vehicles. The men sheathed their shotguns but did not depart.

Ron returned to where his girlfriend and best friend stood waiting. —Here's how they say it is. Blossom Creek Canyon is over that ridge, and Blossom Creek leads back to the major Blue drainage, only on Forest Service land. *Clear* Forest Service land, not checkerboard, so we can go as far as we like from there. But first we've got to drive back and park *outside* their gate. They don't mind us hiking in so long as we park outside their gate and stay on the east bank of the Blue after we cross. They don't want us parking on their ranch or driving through it. We've got to go round.

Pete questioned the arrangement at once —Whatta they got out here they don't want us to see?

*—They say* they're protecting *us. They say* a couple of their bulls are prone to ramming unfamiliar vehicles, might do some real damage to your ride with their horns. Or to us. So these ranchers are looking out for us. *So they say.* Us or your truck, whichever. Both. And for their own liability no doubt. Lots of these folks living out the middle of nowhere worry some hunter or hiker or random lost a-hole is going to come on their land, get hurt and sue them into oblivion. And it does happen. Something like that can break an independent rancher.

This was not their original plan. Their map showed the passable road extending through and somewhat past this parcel. Their goal was always to follow the road till it fizzled, park and hike down the valley beyond all roads and habitation, as far as they got till nightfall, camp one night and double back in the morning. But they'd run late. Too much talk and too many Coronas at the lone saloon in Snowflake then sleeping in till nearly noon and not reaching the road's steep descent into the Blue River's canyon till close to 2:00. The scenery was every bit as spectacular as Pete promised, those rolling blue-green peaks in the west offset by higher rugged blue and purple ranges, the whole of it cut by narrow side canyons left and right. Still, by the time they reached even their failed trailhead it was nearly 4:00. They all three knew dark would drop down early in this deep north-south valley despite the season. No way now they'd make it far before night fell upon them, sudden, deep and dense. . .

The rancher and his man watched wordless as Pete backed his truck onto the road, followed them to the weedy turnout outside the gate across the road from the sign, kept on watching as the trio locked the truck and strapped on their packs. Geared up, they crossed the scrubby strip before the Blue itself, little more than a damp gravel bed here. Once they were over it the hired hand called after them —That's it. Keep on straight up that ridge. Canyon's t'th'other side. You can't miss it you keep goin' straight.

Pete and Ron waved thanks but Sue-Min did not turn back, had no wish to see these men ever again. Once across the diminished Blue they continued up the wide flat ramp of the ridge, convincing themselves they'd caught an actual trail as they picked their way between stunted oaks and twisted pines. As the trees were sparse and their ascent kept them close to the western edge of the ridge, they could look back for some time and still see the two men squatting sidesaddle on their little vehicles, though they soon shrunk to no more than off-white blurs beside the smudge of Pete's old Dodge. Sue-Min missed the moment the ranchers disappeared entire from sight. Their ascent angled, the trees grew too dense, the vehicles and men fell too small from her height. The trio had left behind every contemporary human trace.

The ridge widened while they were unaware so once they reached a level where it grew mostly flat they realized they could no longer scan its full span side to side. The pines were taller here, the low oaks tight in clumps. Postage stamp meadows separated random rock outcrops and jagged bits of ridge. They'd ascended into a patchwork and come sans compass or GPS. Their original plan had been to follow the river, and how could they get lost then? But they'd lost the river, at least for now. Pete thought the canyon must be to their left, as best any of them could remember left. Ron thought they should head back down or at least to the right to relocate the Blue River edge of the ridge. Pete prevailed before either asked Sue-Min's opinion and they all three began meandering toward a hypothetical directionless port, expecting their way always to open onto a new canyon but coming only into more motley oak and pine after each distinctive bit they traversed, Sue-Min damping her emotions down just short of panic. Ron and Pete? If they were worried, she couldn't tell. They all three tramped along, the guys offering random inanities —*At least the weather's good. —I think we're getting close. . .* But mostly in silence.

They'd just come onto a stretch of bare rock strewn with stones when Sue-Min concluded to call for a retreat, but before she could speak up Pete called out —Look at this! It's some kind of pattern!

His words still in her ears, she saw it too, gray stones around softball size set in wandering arcs and arabesques on the granite ground. Several closed cells remained intact though the arms of their neighbors disintegrated at inconsistent lengths. Ron shook his head. —Somebody built this—but who?

Pete's reply struck Sue-Min as ridiculous, asinine —Maybe it was the rancher's kids.

Ron swept three stones over soccer style with the side of his foot, bent to inspect them. —No lichen on their undersides, only above. They've been here a long, long time.

Pete's next reply seemed even more out of whack than his first —Maybe it was a Pueblo.

Sue-Min wanted so bad to get up in his face and yell *These aren't walls! Where's the rest of the stone then? If this is a dissipated site where is the rest of the stone?* Yes, Ancestral Puebloans, Mimbres, or some backwoods branch of the Mogollon had inhabited this canyon, though not right here, not like this. Walter Hough had marked and mapped sites up and down the Blue back before World War I, and Steve Swanson had revisited the area almost a hundred years later. She knew as much, had met Swanson more than once, could share that information, but she had no desire to engage the creeper, let alone antagonize him. Nor to drag things out. She had his number and was maintaining the wall of chill. *Measured, measured. Weighed.* She spoke as little as she could, kept interaction at the barest min.

He must've read something in her gaze though, fixed his own eyes on her expectantly and tilted his head an inch to the left, and after long enough she'd said nothing, gave the least of shrugs, staring at her still. For once Ron came to her aid.

—Hey, look, there's a gap ahead. He pointed beyond their present patch of patterned mystery stones, between the scrub oaks and scraggly pines. Sue-Min and Pete aligned their eyes to his extended finger's course, saw through the dregs of forest to what seemed an empty span. At least a place with no visible trees, little scrub, no upthrust rocks... A shadowed background. Either a seriously major meadow ahead, or Blossom Creek Canyon. *Some* damn canyon anyway...

If it *was* Blossom Creek Canyon then by dropping into it and following its route they should come around and out again onto the Blue—south of the ranch and the ends of all roads, bypass the former altogether.

They funneled together through the gap, Ron taking the lead and never turning back. Once past the pines and onto a stretch of scattered scrub and grass they saw the gash in the earth from some way off. The canyon. A canyon at least. Pete shot forward toward that abyss and almost at once fell hard on his forearms with a rough pained grunt, his foot hooked on some snag invisible in the high grass. He swore without imagination as Ron shuffled up, paying extra attention to his own footing beneath the desiccated thin blades. Pete pushed awkwardly to hands and knees and waved Ron off, palms out —I'm okay, I'm okay. . .

Sue-Min saw smears of blood on both his palms.

Ron offered a similar gesture in response, though with palms angled down and presumably unbloodied. —Okay, okay, just checkin' bro.

Pete turned and staggered into the treeless span. Ron followed after a backward look and a shrug toward Sue-Min. She hitched her pack back up and followed.

A few minutes later they clumped together to a halt at the edge of a canyon. *Blossom Creek Canyon* they hoped. If the ranchers spoke true, this route would take them back to the main trunk of the Blue and its trackless and uninhabited middle stretch. Pete and Ron high-fived without a glance at Sue-Min who stood just a step behind.

Pete sauntered to the edge and the others followed, Sue-Min squeezing between Ron on her left and the branches of a thick twisted fir on her right. Dirt cliffed at the top here, some eighty meters deep and at least that wide a span. Away to their left the canyon boxed off, but not so far ahead it jogged to the right and out of sight. Looked like the east wall rose there and some stone began to show through the slopes of soil. The bottom was a cleft too tight to see.

Descending the dirt wall before them held zero appeal. They saw no paths, no ramps, no natural stairs in the crumbling unstable face, no hand or footholds. Just pink grainy soil, scattered bleached protruding stones, random precarious cacti. Attempting any route down here without rope seemed likely suicide. Even on rope the descent would be sketchy. But a rock face would be different if one were ahead.

Onward then.

Now they at least had a feature to follow. So they followed. They were not lost. *Probably* not anyway. Probably not *yet* anyway. Sue-Min's incipient panic faded some. Pete took the lead again and they picked their way along the ridge, working around standing trees and fallen snags, retreating from the indented edges of scalloped collapse.

The sun where they could see it hovered just above the western slate range in the haze. They held no discussion on the subject, but she knew they all understood they'd have to make plans for night soon. They wouldn't be going much further than this, not today.

They came to the canyon's bend, rounded it. Ahead two changes leapt out at once. From here on, the walls on both sides were stone, steep scoured pink tuff ribbed with dubious holds. In addition their ridge dropped away, grew lower, just as the opposite wall ascended.

They quickened their pace, worked their way down to a less elevated section of the west wall, an almost level grassy area studded with the dark forms of juniper and pines. Across the narrow canyon almost close enough to throw a stone, the east wall—or was it south now?—rose near three hundred meters overhead. The steep stone face was more of the same, scoured and striated and pink, pyroclastic tuff of some sort, ash deposited in strata over how many millennia from what volcano or volcanoes, super or just giant, then cut through by slow eons of flash flood and flow. . .

That was when they saw the cave. Sue-Min was certain she spotted it first, but she only stared in silence so it was Ron who got to point it out and proclaim its presence. Maybe two thirds of the way up the wall and a hundred meters down canyon, a black horizontal oval in the rugged salmon scarp. Ahead of her Pete and Ron conferred close, heads bent together, low excited tones.

—Let's make for that cave. *Ron.*

—Yeah bro, we can camp there. We're gonna need to camp for the night soon anyway. *Pete.*

No shit Sherlock. She knew that already. They *all* knew that already. Probably no bear or mountain lion in there, high as it was. And it was August, not hibernation season yet. So steep though. Her stomach fluttered contemplating the climb, *but fuck it*. She was in better shape than either of the guys.

First they needed to cross. Ron stared from the edge, left-right, down, said —I think we can descend right here, hike up to the cave from below, choose the best ascent there.

—Sounds good to me, bro. Lead on.

Ron looked back at Sue-Min a second, said —Whadda you think, baby? Looks good?

Only he turned before she could answer, dropped to his knees and slid his legs over the edge. Pete followed soon as

Ron was all below. He looked up at her once his head had descended, said —Come on in, the water's fine!

*What an asshole.* She let him climb down at least two full body lengths before she commenced her own descent.

The slope on this side was moderate, the handholds regular and reliable. Soon she reached Pete and Ron at the bottom, or almost at the bottom, wedged between walls only a few feet apart and tapering beneath to a terminal V too tight for traverse, both braced in position with arms and legs splayed out, an awkward pair of mothmen. She wished she'd worn her gloves for this shit. She saw Pete had his on now.

The stagnant murk in the crease beneath their feet could only be Blossom Creek. What they saw of the stream was little more than a foot wide and all but dry, its pitiful arrested trickle of water a black coffee hue. *Oily* black coffee. Only hard rain or snowmelt would make it flow again. Broken branches choked the creekbed's acute angle. She considered how much further each flash flood would propel the jumble of jagged wood, how long some of it lingered in this isolate groove...

They had to chimney along from there, splayed legs and outstretched arms holding them over the creekbed's crevice. It was a familiar caver's maneuver, and they progressed in this peculiar style as if awkward angels.

Below them bleached branches clogged the trench, broken ends awaiting only one missed step to punch through clothes and flesh and draw blood, or just the next flash flood to move them along. She looked upstream at what she could see of the sky. Distant rain would send a torrent toward them even when the sky overhead was blue. No cumulus clouds, no rain. At least so far as she could see.

They made their clumsy way along, hand foot foot hand. Where the cave mouth had to be close to overhead Sue-Min saw forms below like broken rib bones protruding from the opaque water. *Human* ribs. Three curved gray somethings arching up from the coffee hued creek amidst more vegetal forms. And there—wasn't that cracked rod a barely submerged long bone? Once more she took a breath to speak out, but froze.

No way those could be human bones. No way would she give Pete a chance to mock her, think he was bonding that way. Or worse, to offer sympathy if Ron mocked her. Just funky sticks, bones of livestock or mountain goats at most, nothing to see here. . .

Neither of the guys noticed. They pressed ahead until they estimated the cave was right above. The left slope seemed steeper now, nearly vertical. Sue-Min contemplated climbing it wearing her frame pack, how to balance. Yet the alternative was to leave the pack down here, with all her gear, likely to slip into the foul stagnant cola below no matter how tightly wedged. No way to open it here either, take out just those items she might need—and no way to tote that stuff up without a pack if she did. Going up would be all or nothing.

Ron went first, gripping the corroded ridges of tuff, faded khaki pack bobbing on his back as he rose. Pete followed straight off. Sue-Min was ready to go second after Ron, but got no chance. It hadn't taken long for that to become the pattern . . . Ron, Pete, her, repeat.

Her turn came. She all but pressed her breasts against the wall as she took a grip. The rock was not so friable as it appeared, and the thin horizontal ridges cut by ancient floods and flows offered hand and footholds more stable than expected. The slope, though not as extreme as she anticipated, was still steep, and she steeled herself to flatten against it if she slid, avoid tumbling backward and losing all stability. Pressed face forward she might yet regain her grip in a slide.

Somehow they all three made it, crawled and scrambled over a rough rock lip and into the cave. Sue-Min let herself collapse back, panting on the pebbly dusty cave floor with her pack pushed up for an uncouth pillow. Both her hands were sore and torn in several places, and she could feel the palm of her left wet with blood. Ron reclined in a position much like hers, but Pete still stood, though he trembled. She thought already of their inevitable return, whether experience would render it easier on the descent or the change in direction might make it worse. She'd at least dig her gloves out of her pack for that.

Once she got back up and looked around she found the cave was not deep, only a rockshelter really, its rear walls extending nowhere full into dark zone, barely deep enough for permanent twilight at best. The ceiling rose in half a dozen low scalloped domes whose curves extended out to the walls, giving the shelter's interior the look of a dirty compressed cathedral. Its floor area altogether amounted to little more than a good-sized theater stage, especially if all the curtains were drawn.

While the guys unpacked and set up camp she strolled about the hole. Beneath the rear north side dome she found the excised wings of dozens of Catocala moths, strewn in a tight spread little more than one meter round. Hindwings only, some up, some down, like powder-scaly tarots, their insides striped in red and black, outsides black and white. She'd seen this sort of thing once before, in a famous shrine cave near Capitan, New Mexico. The wing scatter marked a spot where bats fed. Or perhaps the work of a single energetic bat.

But no bats hung here. And why only the bright-striped hindwings, evolved to startle birds in flight? Where the drab forewings?

She found the probable culprits over in the final south side alcove, loose cluster of at least two dozen Townsend's big-eared bats, their little charcoal bunny ears poking down within reach, so cuddly she wanted to pet them. But, rabies. It was always a maybe. Not just from a bite—the aerosol of their saliva could spread it alone.

Sue-Min noted the shifting feel of the floor beneath her feet, a sense of gravel grinding. She looked closer at the layer of tiny cobbles covering much of the cave. *River* cobbles. Dusty pebbles two, three, four centimeters around. Rounded, roughly. From the river. Someone hauled them up here a handful at a time. The Mimbres or other Mogollon who worshipped in this place? Why? She knew of prehistoric Southwest cave shrines strewn with pottery sherds in the hundreds, sometimes a thousand or more . . . others stuffed with inordinate numbers of sandals, prayer sticks, cane cigarettes. . . These rounded but dusty river cobbles though? Could this rocky carpet be the remnant of some rain ritual, some offering to ancestors in the watery underworld of night, the rain-bringers who returned as the clouds themselves, came back as the very raindrops. . . ?

Ron called her to where he was making camp. Sue-Min opened her own pack and drew out what she'd need for the night. She forgot to pack a sleeping pad so Ron placed his own under her bag despite the perfunctory protest she made. That settled, they zipped their bags together, creating a single quilted envelope. She smiled at Ron across this square . . . then saw what Pete was doing, what he held. . .

Pete hadn't yet spread his bag out at all. Instead he moved methodically through the cave, a flattened wand coated in gray plastic extending from his hand.

Sue-Min turned on Ron. —No way. You brought me here with a *looter?* Did you not know about this? Tell me you didn't know he was gonna do this. Tell me honestly.

—Aw baby, I didn't think it mattered. He's only looking for Spanish gold, not the stuff you study. Studied. It's a total long shot anyway. Still, Coronado *did* come up the Blue, you know. And they do say he stashed some gold in a cave here somewhere.

—Coronado came here *looking* for gold! He didn't *bring* any!

—Sure he did. He had to pay his men with it. Makes sense he would cache some for the return trip, when he would need it the most.

—You know looters are like my natural enemy, right? Archaeologists hate looters worse than we hate . . . Nazis.

—Well, you're not really an archaeologist, are you? I mean, not anymore, not since they kicked you out.

He looked up at her, seemed to catch the blank stare that paved over her rage and turned away . . . then dared an amendment —And Pete's *not* a looter. He's not looking for *Indian* artifacts. He's only looking for *Spanish* gold . . . or maybe Spanish armor.

Sue-Min's voice came clipped as she answered, precise as a laser —Pothunters, treasure seekers, metal detectorists . . . they're all the same. They trash sites, remove artifacts from their context, erase their provenience, leave them with no connection to their origin, and ruin any data. They destroy our national heritage.

Ron was down on one knee, unpacking items she mostly thought unnecessary—why had he brought four bags of *unpopped* popcorn? He did not look up. Pete meanwhile continued crisscrossing the cave floor, electronic wand angled down around 45 degrees. He swept it in short arcs to either side and ahead, ignoring Sue-Min and Ron.

—You *know* how I hate these guys, and now you drag me out in the middle of nowhere with one? I'm telling you, if he really finds anything I'm shutting him down the second he moves to break the ground!

She had no idea how she'd do any such shutting down unless perhaps Ron backed her up, but thin as Pete's chances were of finding Spanish gold, things would probably never come to that.

Pete doubled back. Apparently he struck out so far. Beelined toward their bedroll till Ron requested he hold.

—Whasamatter, Bro?

—Can you maybe leave off with that thing till morning? Any gold here isn't going anywhere before then. Night's coming down and we should all crash now, get an earlier start than we did today, you know?

Pete shot back a puzzled look and shrugged. He flicked a switch on the detector and let the hand that held it drop to his side, turned and stepped back to his pack to begin spreading his own bedroll.

The cave held no wood except a few dusty twigs, so they built no fire. Instead they chatted across the gap between the sleeping bag islands where they sat, passing Ron's half empty flask back and forth as they spoke. Their prospects for tomorrow, their luck in finding the cave, the strange pattern of the rocks they'd passed. Then Ron changed the topic altogether —When you get down to it those ranchers were decent guys, you know? Real all-Americans, really. I mean, what could be more American than cattle ranchers living down a canyon in Arizona?

Sue-Min hung her head, said nothing, which was fast becoming her routine when Ron was wrong, so she was surprised when Pete replied —Dude, those ranchers were fucking *assholes*. Their story about the bulls was . . . bullshit, and you know it. And don't tell me you didn't see how that one guy was checking out your girlfriend.

Sue-Min was shocked she agreed with Pete for once, but still she held her tongue.

—Duuude. Ron's answer was forced and artificial, hands palms up on his knees in a phony Buddha pose. —Dude. You're just projecting. They're all right.

—Ha! Canyon dwelling inbred weirdoes . . . we'll all be lucky if they're not burying your truck somewhere with their backhoe right this minute.

Ron shook his head. —Chill, man. We'll be fine.

That was it for the conversation, and as the Jack Daniels in the flask was already exhausted, they tugged off their hiking boots, crawled into their sleeping bags, and slipped into sleep, one by one.

Sue-Min woke to a mass crushing her midsection and a beefy hand clamped hard over her mouth. The cave was dark but the reek of sweat and Polo over the low aroma of rock dust told her at once it was Pete. Who the hell even slathers cologne on for a backpacking hike? She sought to struggle but her legs were trapped in the sleeping bag and Pete knelt on her arms so all she could do was thump her knees bluntly against his back through the padding of the bag. She torqued her neck, tried to scan to the sides, but the burly home builder increased his pressure and pinned her head in place. *What the fuck was going on? Where was Ron? How could Pete . . .*

She couldn't see Ron, couldn't see much of anything. Though the cave was shallow its roof was so low no moonlight entered far. Sue-Min squeezed out a short set of stifled squeals, hoping to get her boyfriend's attention or at least wake him if he could somehow still be asleep while his best friend raped her. *Because she knew that's where this was headed.* Any woman would know. Pete had always given off that creeper vibe. She hadn't worried much because Ron was always with her when Pete was around. But where was he now? The first flashes of heart-pounding panic faded and a wintry calm filled her frame in its place. She was going to *survive*. Not only survive. She was going to stop this. Even if she had to hurt him. *Even if she had to. . .* In that moment her mind became icy clear.

She tried to bite Pete's hand but his grip on her jaw covered her chin and was too firm for her to open her mouth. She struggled again to scream but her whimpers dwindled in the back of her throat. Pete shook the shadowed silhouette of his head. His movements seemed at once both frantic and subdued. Something didn't add up. Was Pete himself frightened of something? His face was no more than a blur but she felt certain now he was scared. *Terrified.* Of what—*of Ron?* Where *was* Ron? *Where—?*

Pete was linebacker big, outweighed Ron pretty well and her by maybe double. Sue-Min was no weakling but he was strong and had surprised her. She needed a weapon. What? Her Leatherman was zipped out of reach in her pack. A loose rock might be good but the cave floor offered only a mix of dust and the little river cobbles. A few scattered sticks. If she could find a sharp stick she might stab him in the eye. Worked for Ulysses, right? But his knees pinned her arms at the elbows, her hands already growing numb. Still, if he really wanted at her he would have to get up and peel her bag back at some point. She had to be ready to make her move when that happened. She couldn't expect a second chance.

Sue drew in another breath and Pete pressed her down so hard she could feel individual stones on the cave floor through her sleeping bag and pad and the dense cover of dust beneath. He held his left index finger to his lips to shush her. Then he pointed into the night outside the cave mouth and rolled her head that direction with a shift of his heavy sweaty paw.

She had no clue what he wanted her to see. Outside was just more dark. Then it clicked. Part of the outside was *too* dark. *Far* too dark. She remembered stars when she fell asleep beside Ron, the sky above the opposite ridge thick with them. Now the sky without was a pool of ink. No stars, no moon, no silvered clouds. Nothing.

Pete pointed once more into the night. She understood he was giving directions, asking a question. Asking if she saw . . . *what?* He rolled her head beneath his hand again, pointing out along the angles at the corners of the cave mouth. Left, right, and thin strips of stars there to either side. Pale moonglow on the canyon's facing ridge beneath. Between, more *nothing*. Then she knew this was what he wanted her to see. Something blocked the stars from sight in a broad rising swath straight ahead. Not clouds. Something closer. Some impossible bulk rising from the canyon outside to blot the sky and stars.

Pete held her gaze to the side one more time and pressed his own face forward. She tried to shrink back, expecting he sought to force his mouth on hers, but he only offered the down nod again as he stared at her, his coarse porous face mere inches from her own. He whispered —Promise you won't scream if I take my hand away. If *you* scream, we're *both* dead.

She stared up at him and willed her eyes into Tesla death rays. No luck.

—Listen to me *Sue*. This is life or death. That thing outside, I think it already got Ron. Killed him, ate him, I don't know.

She felt a deep chill emptiness rush through her chest, ice water flooding her guts. Ron. Dead. She already knew—had known it somehow from the moment she woke. Now she was alone with Pete . . . with Pete and whatever was outside. Which was worse?

She struggled to scream again—from grief, from fear, from simple rage—but Pete kept his hand squeezed tight across her mouth. She gasped rapid breaths through his fingers as best she could.

—I want to let you go but you *got* to be quiet. *Promise me.*

Again she beamed back her most concentrated hate. She *never* wanted him on this trip. *Oh, we'll make it a double date* Ron told her. Except Pete's alleged date was a no show, surprise, surprise. If the woman was ever even real. Oh god, was Ron really dead? Then she thought of the vast shadow obscuring the night outside. Oh what the fuck? She managed a stillborn miserable nod beneath his hand. Anything to get him off her. Who would she scream to anyway?

Pete stared down at her, his face suspended so close to her own. She felt certain if they could see each other clearly he would see her hatred and she would see his doubt. She had doubts of her own though. Legit ones. She distinctly felt the rigid root of his cock pressed against her where his crotch splayed over her pelvis, and she remembered from a cultural anthro class how guys were *not* supposed to get hard if they were genuinely scared. Their course text had shown carvings, erect angry effigies from around the world. Ithyphallic. An erection in the face of threat was alleged to demonstrate courage. If Pete wasn't really afraid what else wasn't true? *And what really happened to Ron?*

Still, best to play along at this stage. Getting loose would allow her to call for help, *run* for help, find a weapon, maybe even find Ron. Pinned down this way she had no options, no chance. Nothing.

Again she offered what constrained nod she could, and this time Pete first eased the pressure of his hand then lifted it a few inches above her face. He did not rise off her though and kept close watch on her mouth.

Sue-Min gulped air and turned to the right causing Pete to drop his hand not quite but almost back to her mouth. No Ron in sight. The cave was small, Ron's half empty pack still beside her. Ron was not. Ron was nowhere, nowhere she could see. Outside still the enormous shape of shade, a monstrous blotch of blackness blotting out the night sky. Inside Pete still straddled her, his gaze fixated on her mouth, knees pinning her arms above the elbows, gag hand prepared to clamp down at once if she screamed or yelled, made any sound. He leaned in close and she twisted her head to one side to avoid the unwelcome kiss she still anticipated.

Yet he only whispered in her ear. His voice crackled with what she took for genuine panic. She heard it clear now. *He* was barely keeping it together himself. Which likely made him more a threat.

—Listen to me. If you want to live through this night you *got* to listen to me. Here's what I can tell you. Ron got up. To pee I suppose. I remember that. I half woke as he passed. I looked over at you and you were still asleep. Next thing I know Ron was *gone. Just. Gone.* I got up to check on him and when I came to the edge I saw what was out there. I stayed quiet, backed up slow, *real slow*. I'm sorry I sat on you but I was afraid you would scream and call it down on us if I woke you and showed you without taking measures. There's more to all this but I can't just explain. You've got to see for yourself.

Whoa. All this freaking out over what—a shadow? Was this all a setup? Still, hard-on or no, big burly Pete was visibly upset and she'd never seen him even ruffled before. But was he truly scared? She couldn't deny *something* was bugging him. Plain old-fashioned guilt maybe? What if *he* had done something to Ron. She didn't see how the shadow could be rigged though, and she never pegged Pete for much of an actor, despite his occasional tendency to quote from *Hamlet*. Seriously, what *was* that thing outside? And *where. Was. Ron?*

Pete sank to all fours beside her. She wriggled away fast and as far as the now oversized tandem bag allowed, which was not far. He watched her but let her go.

—Okay. You need to follow me now. Keep low, be as quiet as you can, not a sound. Just trust me—you'll understand when you see. And he swung his incurved arm like a swimmer, like a scythe.

Pete began crawling toward the cave mouth, but Sue-Min's thighs shook so bad she couldn't keep his pace, even after she got free of the sleeping bags. A couple meters on he crooked his neck, looked back at her behind him, barely out from the bag, made mute jerking motions with his chin for her to follow, another inward sweep of his arm. Could he see how she trembled?

She feared to set a precedent by taking his directions in any way, but she knew she needed to see it for herself, whatever *it* was. She steadied her legs some with deep breaths and effort and went on, shuffling over the dusty cobbles in her stocking feet silent as she could.

A few meters from the edge Pete pulled back, chinwagged again for her to go on alone. And again her situation devolved to an undesirable choice. As she crawled past Pete she mouthed —*My choice to go on. My choice, understand?* He only stared back blank as she came to the edge where —*Oh holy fucking shit!*

The dark shapeless form outside rose high above them to where a sort of huge translucent fan crowned it. Some forty meters up or more. Long, broad, veiny . . . *petals* . . . caught the scant moonlight, glinting in oily inconsistency purple red green white blue back to red, marking passage en route through other hues unknown from any crayon box. The colors bore the elusive character of iridescent insects, shimmering back and forth from bright indefinable luminescence to matte absence with a hidden and indefinable rhythm. She gaped at the display, altogether strange yet almost beautiful.

The immense pitch bulk or trunk behind the array seemed immune to the moonlight, showing only as an enormous emptiness in the night. Despite its limited brightness Sue-Min somehow sensed a lack of life in the mass, an overall deadness as if it were a virus or remnant, a thing that lacked any animating spark.

The deathly petalled spread hung overhead like the centerlight pop of a single stillborn firework, one lone frozen moment from a long forgotten Fourth of July. Behind it the unlit trunk rose above and hung below till blocked either way by the cave mouth such that she could not decide the direction of its source, whether it was child of the riven Earth beneath or progeny of the very sky it blocked from view.

Was this great dark thing in the canyon some kind of massive night blooming cactus? Or was she witnessing the manifestation of a gigantic nocturnal beast, perhaps a Godzilla-sized star-nosed mole? Either way where had it been in the light? How could such an enormity simply *appear?*

A muted crunch came from behind. She swung to see Pete on his feet beneath the bat roost, waving his hands in apparent attempt to roust the bats and shoo them out. She heard him whisper —Why aren't you outside? It's night! *Get out!* Get, get! *Go!*

And after all why were the bats still inside this night? That didn't seem right. She pressed herself to the pebbles as they flew overhead, none coming near her. Outside the attenuated moonlight caught the bats as they scattered. They seemed disoriented, flittering in twisted zigzags as if ill till one struck

44

a blade of the object's glimmering fan! She thought she saw the membrane twitch or ripple to intercept the bat, which stuck and hung there and as she watched began to dissipate, the veins glowing brighter right around it. She could see the bat's essence streaming in toward the spread's hidden center through the network of sinuous vessels. Their luminosity increased a moment then diminished and the bat was gone.

Pete stood beside her. She almost gasped but her fear was internal enough for its force to seal her mouth. He moved fast and soundless for a guy his size, even traveling over this gravel. A finger first over his mouth then pointing back into the shallow recess of their meager shelter. He turned, crawled, and she followed.

Opposite where the bats had hung, all the way against the east wall, they were just out of sight of the entrance itself. Pete scrunched down in the farthest spot and Sue-Min did the same, keeping a full two meters space between them to her left though thus forced to leave herself the barest hair in view of the mouth.

Pete turned to her, whispered —The bats . . . did it get any? I wanted you to see.

—Yes. I saw one get stuck and melt. Poor thing.

—I watched the same thing happen to an owl while I was looking for Ron. *Fuck!*

Ron's unwitnessed yet presumably parallel dissolution filled the silence between them.

He didn't open his eyes as he half turned toward her to speak. . . Cocky Pete seemed at a loss for once, for a moment at least, arms hanging loose and head tilted up against the arching wall.

She looked full at him. He'd taken charge since she woke or even before but was he conceding now? After a good two minutes he drew a deep breath and spoke—

—My gut is it'll leave when the sun comes up. Probably just disappear. Fade away back to wherever it came from. We just have to wait it out. Have you got your cellphone?

She shook her head without turning his way. —Left it in the truck. What was the point? No signal out here.

—I know that—It's the *time* I wanna check. What about a watch?

—Ha! Not for years. . .

—I've got a watch but it's too dark to read it. I was hoping you had something digital. He dug out his own phone, flipped up the cover, cupped the screen's glow with his left hand and angled it away from the entrance best he could. —3:37. Does that seem right to you?

—I guess.

—I don't know. It feels wrong somehow. Too late, or too early. Anyway my battery won't last much longer so I'm shutting down to conserve power. We can check the time again in an hour or so. Right now it's all we got. *We* are all we got. Each other. We've got to work together to survive.

Sue-Min hugged herself. She knew *she* was all *she* got, the only one she could trust, and she had to rely on herself. The rest of Pete's ideas made some sense though. Wait and see what happened at sunrise. And if the thing was still there at that point, well at least she would see better what she was dealing with.

—What time does the sun come up? she asked.

—This time of year, 6:00? 6:30 maybe? But we're in a canyon, so it may take another hour or so for it to shine down here.

He stared at her as if expecting her to run calculations in her head and announce the results to contradict him, but she neither replied nor met his gaze. After several seconds passed she felt him turn away.

—We should take turns keeping watch.

—Fine, you first. Her response came without hesitation, and she spun at once and crawled back to her bedroll. She had to think these things through. Lie down, maybe rest. Maybe sleep through it all if she could, wake come morning, deal with what was left to deal with then. From one side she heard Pete's mumbled —Okay. I'll wake you after what I think is an hour.

—How about you don't wake me *at all* unless it's life or death, or you find some sign of Ron. Turning away from Pete once more she bent and gripped the matched edges of the tandem bedroll she and Ron had shared, hands splayed wide as leverage allowed, dragged it toward the cave's back wall as far as she could get from Pete, though careful not to disturb the moth wing Sargasso.

Once arrived at this terminus she wriggled down inside the sack, back against the wall, head bent on bended knees, not caring if Pete witnessed her undisguised display of weakness.

She crouched and cried in silence. Thoughts of the thing outside never left. Thoughts of Ron never left. Sleep refused to come. Her tears oozed in slow soundless streams. She knew it was in no way logical but she felt abandoned, so much so she wanted to curse Ron for whatever stupid thing he must've done to draw the monster's attention. She pictured him cocky enough to try talking to it, same as he had with the ranchers. He thought he could talk to anyone if he knew even two words in their language—French and German tourists, an old Navajo couple in a truck stop near Thoreau, the waitress at a Greek restaurant in Albuquerque. Those occasions were awkward at best. Worst of all was when he tried speaking to her in broken Korean. That always ended in a fight. Could he have imagined himself a monster-whisperer?

More likely though he just staggered groggy and clueless to the cliff edge and unzipped, little LED light on his forehead, and then what? Maybe the thing snatched him up right then. Maybe it hadn't and Ron simply stumbled and fell when he saw it. Either way, wouldn't he have yelled? Why hadn't they heard? The canyon's acoustics? Perhaps Pete *had* heard and that's why *he* woke up. Or perhaps Pete had been there too. Perhaps Pete had pushed Ron. Would she really put that past him? Perhaps it was not an owl Pete saw dissolving but Ron . . . maybe Pete actually offered Ron up as some sort of sacrifice. . .

Maybe Pete had known this thing would appear outside tonight, *known it all along . . . maybe that was why he brought them here.* Why hadn't he sacrificed her too then? Was it because he wanted her for himself? How would the monster feel about that? Could she somehow offer Pete in *her* place? Would the thing let her go if she gave it Pete? What were the protocols for offering a sacrifice? Just pushing him from the edge didn't seem enough. Did she need to know some ritual, a chant, wave a crystal or a magic staff? In any such case she was fucked.

It wasn't fair to Ron for her to feel abandoned. Not if he really were dead. What if he were still alive somehow though, trapped perhaps on the opposite edge of the canyon, trying to get back to them. If the monster disappeared and she left at sunrise, wouldn't *she* be abandoning *him?* She remembered her birth mother handing her a worn and sweat-stained *Hanji* doll before retreating forever down a plain gray hall, not looking back, other women coming to fawn over Sue-Min, complimenting the doll, saying how lucky she was in a language she no longer spoke but still partly understood, sometimes heard in her dreams. She remembered that doll, its white smiling face, its tiny red kissy mouth. But she had no memory of it past that moment. What happened to the doll? When had she lost it—or when had it left her, who took it away? Had it even traveled with her out of Korea? She'd been nearly four then. Her next major memories were American TV, animal shows mostly—*Flipper, Lassie, Big Ben.* She needed one of those friendly entities to rescue her now, chase Pete away and lead her to safety past the creature in the canyon.

But no animal helper came. She was all on her own here. And she knew it.

Her mind cycled through every level of consciousness except sleep. She might as well have been cranked up on caffeine. Sleep was not going to come easy, not any time soon.

After what felt like several hours but was probably less than twenty minutes—and just as she slipped into sleep's first light stages—she felt Pete's hand on the back of her neck, his breath on her cheek. That awful sweat and Polo smell. She stiffened before he could speak, shook his hand off and wriggled away, the zipped together bags bunching about her right elbow and foot.

—What the fuck Pete? What do you want?

—Nothing. I just thought . . . you know . . . we're all alone here . . . and we may not make it out . . . I saw you shaking, like maybe you were crying . . . I thought I should hold you, help you get through the night.

—I don't need your help.

—I thought I could comfort you.

—We're not Adam and Eve here Pete, so don't get any ideas. If you were right before and this thing outside belongs to the night, then we're only trapped a few hours longer, and soon as the sun comes up we can make tracks back to our everyday world, contact the police or the Forest Service or whomever to come look for Ron. *If* we don't find him on the way out. . .

She felt his hand again, harder, tighter, thumb and fingers almost encircling her left bicep, even through the bag.

—Sue. . .

—My name is Sue-*Min*. Sue. Min. Let me go.

—Listen, Sue.

She struggled to pull free again but this time he tightened the cables of his fingers round her arm through the layered bag, squeezed.

—Listen Sue. We're trapped here at least till daylight. Maybe longer. Might be we're both gonna die here. We could help each other pass the time, help each other get to sleep.

—Pete, *please* just let me go, okay? She spoke in a strained whisper. In response he gripped her tighter, dragged her closer across the coarse cobbly floor.

—C'mon, don't be that way. Ron's not here, he's prob'ly dead. And I seen the way you look at me.

—Seriously? *How* do I look at you?

—You know, like—

She cut him off. —You know what? I *avoid* looking at you. And she knew right there she made a mistake. She had *engaged*. Offered an opening for his distorted reasoning.

—Yes you do. I seen you checking me out. You're sly, but I know you wanna give me some of that Asian persuasion. . .

Oh shit. At once she came wide awake, scattering any stray petals of Morpheus from her brain. Pete had crossed a line, and from here on she had to be not just hostage but hostage negotiator, had to argue her own release. But even successful where would she go? Pete had played his hand. Now she had to buy time, bluff.

—Don't you think we should focus on this thing outside, on survival? We shouldn't be looking for new ways to draw its attention.

She could name what Pete was angling toward, but that felt dangerous in itself. Best to leave some uncertainty around her recognition of his intent, degrees of doubt, not admit they were even discussing . . . *that*. She was certain Pete would take any overt mention of sex as a sign of deeper connection, an invitation.

She felt his hand slide up to her shoulder as he craned his head to look at her.

—What's wrong with you? You're Asian. Aren't you people supposed to be submissive?

She bit back an exasperated scream. *No confrontation.* In an argument he would sooner or later find reason for turning to force. And the thing outside might hear their scuffle. She calmed herself best she could then proceeded with her stock response to this and other stereotypes —Okay, first of all, I *am* from Korea, but I was *raised* here. Just like you. *This* is my culture.

—What difference does that make?

Was he that dense, or was he consciously attempting to escalate, goad her into giving his threadbare conscience the provocation it required to increase his level of physical aggression? She needed a distraction.

—What do you know about the Korean War?

—Same as Nam, right? We fought the commies. Except we broke even in Korea, didn't lose the whole enchilada.

She cringed but continued —How much do you know about the side effects of the war—of any war?

—Casualties. MIAs. My grandfather lost his best friend in that one.

—Yeah, but do you know what war does to children?

—They didn't have child soldiers back then. Did they?

—I'm not talking about child soldiers. I'm talking about international adoptees. Do you know anything about them?

—You're talking about Korean kids?

His ignorance gave her a chance to assert a fragile authority. —Orphanages in South Korea were overcrowded and understaffed even before the Armistice. War orphans, G.I. babies. . . Then this missionary couple got the idea of offering the children up for adoption in the U.S. The Holts. They adopted eight Korean babies and wrote a book about it, started their own adoption agency. Holt International. The whole thing really took off from there. It was practically a fad for a while. Over two hundred thousand Korean children were expatriated altogether. An entire lost generation.

—What's all that got to do with anything? It's ancient history. I'm talking about now.

—It has to do with now. It has to do with *me*. I am one of those kids.

—You were adopted?

—*Obviously enough*. Not one of the Holt kids—I came over later, in '71, and not as a baby, not from an orphanage—I was old enough I can remember my birth mother a little. I remember when she left me, gave me up. I didn't understand. Still don't understand. On some level I hate her. But I still love her too. How can I *not* love her—she's my mother? And I love my adoptive parents. How do you reconcile that? I don't even try, not anymore.

By way of response he rolled fast on top of her, pinning her legs once more with his bulk, his speed such she had no chance to react. He slid his left hand underneath her head, torqued her face toward the opening and the vast mass fixed outside in the night. —*That!* Look at that! We've got no time for flashbacks, for *This Is Your Life*. We've got life or death right outside. So what you're adopted? Big deal. Be glad you got to come to America, greatest country on Earth. American soldiers died to bring you that freedom.

—You think Korea is third world? *I've been there.* In some ways it's more advanced than the U.S.

—What are you trying to say? If you're gonna bash America, I don't fuckin' wanna hear it.

—What I'm telling you is whatever you think about Asian women doesn't apply to me. Whatever you think about *Korea* doesn't apply to me. Whatever you think about *Korea* doesn't apply to *Korea! Whatever wrongheaded racist bullshit,* but she didn't say that part aloud. —Please get off me Pete. Please? Her words came out as a wheeze because of the bulk he pressed against her chest. She could feel him twisting to align his hips above hers, his erection returned and already grinding her hip. She groped in vain along the floor for a weapon to jab in his eye but here too the cave offered nothing but pebbles. Any more likely item was still in her pack or Ron's.

—*Pete No!* Her compressed stage whisper came out almost loud enough to echo, but he hesitated less than a second at the sound. He did hesitate though. She didn't miss that. He was fully on her now, hands reaching for the edges of the sleeping bag to tug it down. As she fought back panic a last inspiration came.

—Stop or I'll scream and that thing will hear us! Won't it? I think you know somehow. You know more about that thing than you're letting on.

At once he clamped his hand over her mouth again, slid his hips over hers altogether. She could feel his erection against her belly now. Hard as it was, his cock felt small—compared to Ron's anyway—and Ron's was only average. She didn't want to feel any more of Pete's than she felt this moment.

Sue-Min struggled best she could, sought to squeeze out a scream between Pete's thick-linked fingers. No luck. Her breath hissed heavily through her nose. The way he held her she could barely move.

Pete's free hand slid across her chest, groped at her breasts, left then right, his attempt grotesquely clumsy since she'd unsnapped her bra when she first lay down with Ron and it still hung loose beneath her shirt, cups crumpling under Pete's fingers and frustrating his efforts to reach her nipples. He arched off her a fraction as if to give himself room to maneuver. She floundered as he fondled her but proprioception identified her only free move as toppling to her right—which did not seem advisable as it would allow him to pin her facedown to the pebbly floor.

Pete fumbled for the metal snap at her waistband now, and this required him to rise off her a bit more. Within that interval she brought her arms up, pressed forearms to his chest and shoved hard, and once he lost his balance and flailed, she used his body for leverage to rise and jerked her legs from under him as well. He fell back as she shot up, only to catch her feet in the sleeping bag so she tumbled almost right back on top of him. He flailed his left arm across her chest but she rolled away, pulling free of the bag, ended on all fours several feet from Pete. Without thought she scrambled toward the cave mouth, ignoring the pain as the more jagged of the river pebbles dug under her kneecaps, into her palms. Pete rolled over as well and came after her. This time *she* was faster. A meter from the dripline she spun and flopped on her haunches, pointed both index fingers at her open mouth, said loud as she dared —*Come any closer and I will scream!* Pete froze where he was, a few feet off, still crouched on all fours.

—This is *not* happening. It is not! She spoke with authority despite the continuing quaver in her voice. —Now back up against the wall or I. Will. Scream! *I will!*

—C'mon Sue . . . you don't wanna do that!

—My name is Sue-*Min* you asshole, and don't tell me what I want to do. I'll tell *you* how it's going to be from here out. Now back up into that south corner of the cave, past where the bats were.

Whatever Pete did or did not know about the hearing and habits of the thing outside, it appeared the threat of her scream held genuine sway over him. She knew it was likely a doomsday weapon, mutual assured destruction, but he seemed genuinely afraid she would deploy it.

—Okay, okay. Just don't do anything stupid. And he actually began backing toward the corner just like she directed him, resembling some squat wretched sea creature on his hands and knees. If she could read his face in the gloom, what would she see revealed? Anger? Resentment? Guilt? Confusion? Fear? A mix perhaps, though she guessed mostly fear. She'd struck on something. But how long could she extract leverage from her threat?

Pete backed up, passive aggressive and slow, but after a couple minutes he reached the wall in the corner. There he sat and leaned his head against the stone's coarse arc, his eyes aimed toward the low domed roof.

Sue-Min brought her knees up and hugged them to her chest as if to muffle the sound of her galloping heart. This position helped some to still the tremors that shook her. How impossible could her situation be, trapped between a rapist and something a thousand times larger? She'd achieved a stalemate with Pete for the moment, but how long would it last? Certainly he'd be on top of her if she nodded off half a minute. Thought of the vigil she would have to maintain turned her empty stomach acid. Adrenalin had helped her thus far, still held her, and now it brought rage.

—Did you call that thing up, Pete? Did you summon it here?

His hesitation registered to Sue-Min as surprise... surprise she guessed the truth? Surprise at her accusation? Surprise a 114 pound woman got the better of him, backed him down? What had he done to women before, other women who had no threat to hold over him, no weapon for protection?

He didn't answer, simply stared upward. Not as if she expected a reply.

His silence made her nervous though, so she took a different tack —What's your phone say now?

He continued to stare at the stone ceiling for maybe five Miss'ippi, then pulled the phone from his pocket and flicked it on. After a minute its pale glow coated his face and he read aloud —4:19. We've still got a ways to go.

A pause.

—I wasn't going to hurt you, you know. Just the opposite. I could make you feel happy, help you forget this situation. Help us both. *If* you weren't so fuckin' uptight. How come you got to be such a bitch?

She considered his insult, its definition as he saw it—*bitch, (n)—any woman who declines sex with any man any time.* Her reply was simple—she pointed again at her mouth with one hand, gestured toward the entrance with the other. As loud as she dared yet soft as she could she said —I *will* scream. Pete was barely a vague blur now, but she could sense the tension in his folded arms. Nod off for a minute though, and that's all he would need.

And outside was the creature, the thing, the unimaginable enormity that presumably devoured Ron. She sat now with her back to it. On its very doorstep even. This was not the best thought out plan, but she hadn't had a whole lot of time to think. Pete had forced her to act and she had acted. Maybe she was lucky to be where she was. Or maybe she'd only scrambled out of the frying pan *Fuck oh fuck oh fuck this was all so wrong.* Yet except for the monster, it was nothing new in her life—how many times had she escaped one toxic relationship only to hurl herself into the arms of another? And creepy guys pulled this shit on her all the time.

The thought struck her—not for the first time—there was a discontinuity between her image of herself as independent, a free spirit, and her tendency to slide from one relationship right to the next. To define herself through relationships. Bad ones.

Ron, though . . . Ron was different. Not perfect—he could be neglectful, especially around Pete or his other male friends. *Especially around Pete.* Why Ron felt the need to impress this guy so much she did not understand, but in the three months they'd been dating she often took a backseat to Pete. She'd come to see it as the price she paid to be with a guy who didn't hurt her, didn't hit her, didn't talk down to her. Seemed to like her for who she was, not for the shape of her eyes, her nation of origin. Never said *Five dollah make me hollah* when he wanted to fuck. She'd actually been with guys who waved a fiver at her in the bedroom and thought they were funny. More than a couple. She could picture Pete pulling that trick. But not Ron.

Adrenalin faded and she already felt drowsy, despite the menace behind and the menace ahead. She might as well talk to Pete, make conversation. At least that way she'd know he was also awake.

—What else did you see outside? Did you see what that thing did to Ron?

No answer.

—What about this cave? Did you know it was here before we started out? Was this your destination the whole entire time?

No answer.

—C'mon Pete. You said we've got to work together to survive. If we're supposed to be a team, don't you think you can at least tell me the truth? How much of this did you plan ahead?

At last Pete broke his silence —You think you're so smart.

—No. . .

—Yes you do. You think you're like Charlie Chan's Number One Daughter. I'll tell you what—you don't know a goddamn thing. You can't see inside my mind.

—Trust me, I don't *want* to see inside your mind. . . All I did was ask you a couple questions.

—Well, they're stupid questions. How 'bout you focus on how we're gonna get outta here, okay?

She risked a glance over her right shoulder, up the wall of darkness to the shimmering pinwheel overhead. It seemed closer now, such that she viewed the veiny array almost from its lower edge. She turned farther, halfway round. The sections of the tremendous fan resembled the blades of a windmill, though its blades or petals were more numerous and didn't spin, only rippled a bit in a breeze she could not feel. Captivating, fascinating, like seaweed beneath a shallow sea. She found it hard to look away. She had to.

She spun back toward Pete. He'd made no move closer but seemed poised now, knees arched and knuckles pressed against the gravelly cave floor.

That was how it was going to be. All the way to sunrise at least. She needed a string with bells. Or a fence, preferably electric. And if she did doze off, would she awake as she fell? She needed some siren, some alarm, something that would go off if her grip relaxed. A sound grenade. The problem with those ideas was they would likely call the thing down on her. That and they were impossible from the start.

—What else do you know about this thing, Pete?

He turned to her slow. —Not a damn thing.

—Sure you do. You know it hunts by sound.

—I never said that.

—But you're scared of noise attracting it.

—Maybe I'm just being careful—like you should be.

—We've got to pass the time for a couple more hours at least. Why don't we play a game?

—Oh, what, like *I spy with my little eye maybe . . . something beginning with F—fucking giant monster?*

—I don't know, I thought more like charades.

—Please, Sue-*Min*, could you just try and keep quiet, and not make any sudden gestures?

—So you *do* know something about this thing and its habits. . .

—I'm just trying to be cautious. Maybe *you* could try too.

—Maybe I should've been more cautious when you were trying to rape me, how about that?

—Ha! You know you want it. Even now when you're playing hard to get. It's not rape when you're into it.

—How the hell am I into it?

—*You've been coming on to me from Day One.* I left you alone till now out of respect to Ron, but Ron's gone and we may not live to see the morning ourselves, so why not stop playing games and enjoy what time we have?

—How do you know for sure Ron's gone? Did you see what happened to him?

—He's not here. Where else would he be? Do you think he'd run away on us? Head back to the truck alone and leave us behind to deal with this craziness?

—Ron wouldn't do that. But now she wondered—could Ron still be alive? Had he found time to escape when the thing first appeared outside? Could it be he was going for help even now? But Ron didn't have the truck keys—far as she knew they remained in Pete's pocket. Who could he ask for help—the ranchers? They might just as likely shoot him on sight if he came knocking on their door at night. Ron wasn't leaving the canyon then.

She saw Pete nod in the gloom. —That's right. Where would he go anyway? Good luck with those ranchers. They wanted to shoot us the first time. How do you think they'd react if any of us showed up outside in the middle of the night?

—Let's change the subject. We don't know for sure where Ron is, so we shouldn't get carried away. Maybe he's waiting at the truck. Maybe he's trapped across the canyon. Maybe we'll find him in the morning.

—No, let's be real here. Ron is *gone*. Gone, gone, gone. Most likely *dead*. One way or another he ain't coming back. It's time for you to face that fact.

—You don't know that!

—It's obvious! How can you ignore it?

—Because I know Ron better than you.

—Oh really? Is that what you think? Who's known him since grade school? Who knows the name of the girl he lost his virginity to and where it happened? Who taught him how to shoot a .45? Who's lost count of the backcountry hikes we've taken together—up till now all without you?

As he said this Pete had begun to crawl forward on knuckles and knees. He moved slowly as if he thought she would not notice that way.

—Whoa right there Pete. Whoa and back up.

He froze but held his position, several feet forward of where he'd been before he began his little monologue.

—I'm only going to say this once. *Go back to the wall where you were before.*

He didn't move. She began to count in her head, wondering would she scream at ten, at twenty? She wasn't sure. She wasn't sure she could do it, trade a known threat for an unknown. The important thing though was for Pete to believe she would.

At twelve he hesitated, lurched and crawled back to the wall in reverse. Once he reached it she continued the conversation as if he never moved.

—Just because you've known him longer doesn't mean a thing. Who makes pillow talk with him? With whom does he share his deepest fears? Who knows his dreams? Do you know how he got that scar high up his right thigh? Do you know where his mother moved after she left them? Did you ever suck his cock? I doubt it. I know how he acts, what he'd do in this situation.

But *did* Ron have a chance? Or did that thing outside snap him up before he knew what got him? Slow streams of tears oozed down each of her cheeks. Perhaps their argument had no purpose other than to make her cry. She knew Ron was dead, despite all her hopes. She didn't know if Pete could see her crying, but she didn't dare look away. That might be a giveaway as to her emotional state, and if he saw her as vulnerable he might take it as another opportunity to advance. She knew now how fast he could move. He was in excellent shape.

She fought her tears back till she thought she could speak clearly and returned to their conversation. —Look, Pete, let's not fight. It's not helping.

—No shit.

—Yeah, well I agree with you we've got to work together. We should talk about how we're going to get out of here.

—We're not going anywhere as long as that thing's outside. At least I'm not. You can do whatever you want I guess, but personally I'd prefer to have a witness when I tell this story to the police or the FBI or whoever. It's going to be way worse if I come back alone.

He had a point there. She imagined herself the sole survivor, telling the story to some detective in a gray room with a two-way mirror. Mental hospital, jail for life—that's how a lone survivor would likely end up. She considered again the possibility that Pete somehow sacrificed Ron to the monster. If he'd thought out the aftermath it would explain why he left her alive. One explanation anyway. Was it even the kind of monster that accepted sacrifices? And if it did, would that make it a god? She wondered what wishes or prayers it granted in response to a successful sacrifice. Wasn't Pete already looking for a pot of gold? Was this his plan to get it?

All this sacrifice stuff was pretty far out though. It was hard to picture Pete as any kind of priest or wizard. And what did she know about monsters anyway? Probably Pete's original story was true, how he'd gone to the cave mouth looking for Ron and spotted the gigantic night-obscuring thing instead. In that case she maybe should be grateful it hadn't been her— she might've rushed up there shouting Ron's name and that would've been the end for her *and* Pete as well. Disintegrated like the bat. Or maybe worse. Who knew what the unseen parts of this enormity might do, what claws and jaws were hidden in its shadow?

—Hey. Pete spoke in a stage whisper. —Hey.

—Hey what?

—Why don't you come away from the entrance. You're going to attract that thing's attention. I don't think it even knows we're here so far. You don't need to be that close to the edge.

When she didn't respond he added —I'll stay right here. I promise I won't touch you.

—Yeah right.

—Honestly. Cross my heart and hope to die.

—Maybe you shouldn't hope that out loud.

—Whatever. Come away from the edge. It's not safe for either of us, you being there.

So far Pete's advice, his grasp of the situation, had actually been good. *Except for the attempted rape and all.* But he seemed to understand the monster situation. His plan to wait till morning made sense. If the thing didn't fade away with sunrise, they'd at least get some better sense of its dimensions, maybe spot some escape route or weakness. The ranchers might even report them missing if they didn't return to their truck by the end of the day. Or not—she pictured the hired hand using a backhoe to bury their truck in a trench. Next to a dozen others, all the way back to Model T's. . .

—Oh shit. *Don't move.*

Damn. What was Pete pulling now?

—Wha—?

—Shhh! Don't say anything, *and don't turn around.* There's something behind you.

Seriously? Just when she was ready to grant him a smidge of credence, he had to go and spring the oldest trick in the book? Yet he spoke slower and slightly louder than before, as if to give his words more gravity. And wasn't the point of that trick to *make* her turn around? Had Pete messed up his scheme or was there really something. . .

She turned. And saw the new thing approaching. Was it a *thing,* or an *effect?* An *event?* She could not be sure. It didn't help she'd turned from the wrong shoulder so she had to twist further at the hips to see it better. Now she was sideways to

Pete, facing away, an alarm bell ringing in the back of her brain so long as he was out of sight.

Drifting in the air behind her came a . . . ripple. A blur. She lacked the words. Approximately twice the span of her torso, the whatever it was had no distinct outline or shape. Or color. It hovered and twisted up the limited light like the air over heated pavement, the view through fountain glass. Not that there was much to see beyond the distortions themselves. It was as if a translucent flag drifted on its own, free of any pole, flapping in a nonexistent breeze.

Then as if she'd made eye contact or somehow caught its attention, it locked on a course and approached. She thought to scuttle backward but her muscles refused to respond. In seconds the region of ripples reached her . . . and passed right through her, so far as she could tell. She felt nothing as it struck, but immediately after she was convinced her flesh bore a coat of flat waxy scales, even beneath her clothes. She glanced at her bare forearms, saw nothing, ran her hands down them, felt nothing. By then the impression was gone.

She spun and saw the ripple or disturbance hovering some two meters past her, advancing no farther. Pete was huddled as far back in the cave as he could manage.

—Pete. Hey, Pete.

He did not respond.

—Pete, it's safe. It went right through me and I barely felt a thing. Don't worry.

He didn't answer, didn't move. She could see his face but couldn't tell if he was watching her or the drifting ripple. It hung a bit to the north, didn't seem interested in Pete at all—at least not yet. As she watched he raised his left hand just a few inches slowly and pointed toward her again. Then he hissed out one word —Others.

Sue-Min spun again and this time had to throw her left hand down to keep from losing her balance. It slid a few inches through the little cobbles till it found purchase then held.

Now she glimpsed a scatter of pinkish hovering blobs, varying in size but all smaller than her head. A dozen, maybe two dozen. They advanced slowly, swirling about each other, swelling and distending, dumbbell to sphere to sausage and back. Flattening into discs. Other shapes. Flashing pink to gray. When they reached the entrance they passed all around her on either side. None of them struck her or even came close.

Pete continued staring in what she presumed was terror—at the ripple, at the oncoming blobs, at her—she could no way tell. Once inside the little cave the blobs wandered about while the ripple came to rest above the graveyard of moth wings. One blob drifted toward Pete and he contorted to avoid it, slouched backward to his elbows, almost to the ground. It exhibited no interest in him, stretching to a cylinder before reaching the wall above him instead and blinking out as it struck. But not quite all at once—it seemed to suck into the stone like a sloppy eater's spaghetti noodle. As she watched, the blobs all met the walls or floor or ceiling and disappeared one by one. One of the last wandered back, and before she could dodge, it struck her left shoulder. This time she felt a faint dampness, and the feeling lingered longer than the waxy sensation she experienced earlier.

The second the last blob was gone the ripple blinked out as well, sudden and complete, like a flat screen TV blinking off for the night.

The feeling of damp in her shoulder remained, though fading. She ran her hand over her shirt but it felt dry.

She found herself shaking. Maybe it was the encounter. Maybe it was just the early morning chill—no matter where you were, desert or jungle, it got really cold right around 4:00 a.m. Fieldwork taught her that. New Mexico, Utah, Turkey, Belize—always the same, that's when the chill came. It was cold like that right now, which at least had to mean the dawn was almost upon them. She looked at her sleeping bag crumpled against the wall. If she started to shiver it was going to be hard to stop.

She brought her knees up, hugged them again to her chest. —Well Pete, you're the expert. Any idea what those things were?

A long moment passed before he answered —I dunno. Pause. —They must have something to do with the thing outside. Its breath, its spit, something it sheds? Its babies, its eggs? Some kind of parasites that slid off its skin? Hallucinations it caused us to see?

—Two of them hit me. The big flickering thing and one of the blobs. They all went right through me. I felt them though. I can still kind of feel where the blob hit. It feels wet but it's not. Whatever they were I don't think they were hallucinations exactly. Not the way I felt them.

—Whatever they were I think you attracted them sitting where you are. I wish you would come away from there before you attract something worse.

—I already did. I attracted *you*. Better I take my chances with this monster and its friends.

—Don't talk that way Sue! I'm not like that! I swear. *I swear on my mother's grave.* I swear on the American flag. If you come back here I *will* leave you alone. No means no, *I get that*, I know. I was lonely, that was all. And scared. I admit it, I was scared. I'm still scared. We're both scared. Not all men are what you think. I just had a bad moment. I'm OK now. You're safe with me.

—I'm scared of *you*, don't you get that? And I have very good reason.

She couldn't see his facial expression but she saw him hang his head. Bullshit acting.

—I'm sorry. I'm really sorry. Please come back this way. I won't touch you again. But we'll both be safer if you come away from the cave mouth. That much I'm sure of.

She regarded his vague huddled form in the rear of the space, tried to gauge his sincerity, his acting ability, the ratio of one to the other. His fear, hers. *A leopard doesn't change its spots*, something her adoptive father used to say. Fear could do a lot though.

Sue-Min glanced outside and up. Was the bat-melting blossom really closer now, larger? How much longer before it reached out for her? Her gut told her Pete was right at least about the danger of her location. Hadn't Ron most likely attracted its attention simply by standing in this very spot? She envisioned the pinwheel dipping and spinning, licking her up with a flick of one immense petal. . .

—Please Sue-Min? Please come away from there.

She waited, considered, weighed her fears. —Okay. First off you understand I'll scream as loud as I can *the second* you come near me, right?

—Yeah, no problem, I'll leave you alone, just like I said. I swear.

—Second, you need to move as far as you can into that sort of alcove behind you.

He immediately began wriggling the final few feet into the last rounded extremity of the shelter. He had to hunch just a little once he was all the way in.

She took a deep breath, said —All right. Not one move or I will scream like nothing you ever heard before.

—Yeah, yeah, okay. I get it. Just come away from the entrance.

She began to crawl toward the rear of the cave, the dusty cobbles wedging beneath her kneecaps again. She wished she had her kneepads in her pack, but she hadn't expected to do any caving on this hike so she'd left them behind. Not that this dinky rockshelter with no real dark zone counted as a genuine cave. She kept Pete in the corner of her eye the entire time, flicked glances at him every few feet.

At the wall she considered her sleeping bag. Her bag and Ron's, still zipped as one. She eyeballed Pete, looked back at the bag, decided not to slither inside. Instead she sat in the gravel with her back to the wall and tugged the bag up over her knees to her neck, smoothed it down along her sides. She wasn't going to get trapped again. Using it as a blanket, if she had to she could jettison it as a decoy, a distraction, like squid ink, a lizard's tail. If he just didn't get hold of her head or her hair. . .

—You stay there now.

Through the gloom she saw him cross himself. —Cross my heart. I swear.

Too much adrenalin coursed through her yet to sleep. That and she knew she needed to pee soon. Which had been a problem the entire trip. Earlier she at least had Ron to keep lookout. Now? She could retreat to the corner opposite from Pete—or the entrance—but she had no way to keep him from staring at her all the while. She tensed at the thought of squatting, watching out for Pete spying on her, and trying to get low enough not to spatter. She'd almost rather pee guy style over the edge and take her chances with the monster.

And what about Pete? How long before he too needed to pee? Would he somehow exploit that necessity as an opportunity to expose himself to her—and that exposure to initiate something worse? Their situation made the simplest things suddenly unpleasant and complex.

She could wet herself under her cover, but she wasn't ready to go that far just yet. If they got out of here they were presumably going to the police or a ranger station, and she didn't want to go like that. Jeans pee-stained and reeking would not be an asset to her credibility. She considered her options. Pee herself where she sat. Pee at the entrance, which was probably how that thing got Ron. Get as far from Pete as she could to pee, which would not be far in this little cave.

She clenched against an urge fast becoming a throbbing ache, knowing she could hold it only so much longer before the choice would be made for her. Not much longer.

After several minutes fidgeting she turned slowly toward Pete. Just then Pete spoke —I've got to take a leak, and I don't want to go up to the edge, not with that thing out there. Will you look away till I'm done? I'll do the same for you if you want me to. Promise.

That was unexpected. But he sounded sincere, so far as she could tell. As if *she* wanted to watch *him* anyway. . . Of course he could always rush her if she looked away. And why *shouldn't* she go first? Then again, if he took his turn without doing anything weird, wouldn't she feel safer addressing her own need? After a moment to ponder she said —*Okay, deal*, and faced to her right, cheek pressed against the vaguely moist rear wall of the cave. —Just tell me when you're done, okay?

She heard his boots grind over the pebbles, then faintly his stream as it spattered the wall. She pictured him trying to write his initials or some stupid thing, but knew that probably wasn't true. He spoke before he was done —Oh shit.

—What? She answered but did not turn.

—It just hit me. Arizona doesn't *do* daylight savings time. It's still an hour earlier here.

—What time is your phone set to? Mountain or Arizona? It doesn't matter unless you changed it for here.

—No. It's still set for Albuquerque. Mountain.

—Then sunrise should be around when we're expecting it. Pause. —Can I turn around now?

Faint, she heard him zip up. —Yeah, yeah, go ahead. I'm done.

—Check your phone. What's it say?

She turned now, watched him struggle to dredge the device from his pocket. Then he found it, flicked it open and thumbed it on. And waited. For nothing. —It's dead.

He tucked it back in his pocket and slumped as he sat, for several seconds his outline dissolving even further in the shadows, and then he came straight again sudden enough to make her jerk backward even though he was nowhere close.

—I'm going to get something out of my pack, okay? I promise I won't come near you, so stay cool. I'll go over, get it out, and come back here. No screaming, okay?

She could tell he was watching her, waiting.

—Okay. But go slow. Only not too slow. Get it done and go back.

He began to crawl toward the pack. She pushed back against the wall as far as she could go. It was only once he'd actually begun to rummage in his pack that she remembered he might have a gun. She sucked in a gasp just as he held up his prize.

—Got it!

—Got what? If he had the Glock out, she didn't want to play games. Best to establish new ground rules right away. They both knew he wouldn't dare shoot it here.

—Glowstick. He began to back up toward his corner.

Something drained from inside Sue-Min and she almost laughed. A spasm ran through her and she had to fight off the shakes, but when she realized he still might've got his gun out too, ice water welled up to refill the vacuum within her and she calmed.

When she looked over she saw the cold green glow already defining Pete's face, his knees up to block the light from the cave mouth all he could. Then he shook his head. —*What the fuck?*

—What?

—My watch says *9:12. No way* is that right. We haven't been here *that* freakin' long. The sun would be up, it wouldn't matter *what* time zone, *what* canyon we're down.

She struggled to process this new frustration. The only timepiece left to them and it had run amok. Nothing was working right. Everything was breaking down. On top of that she still had to go. *Now.*

—Okay, so while you're figuring that out, it's my turn to pee. Will you do the same for me?

—The same what?

—As I did for you. Promise not to watch while I pee.

Several seconds of silence then —Yeah yeah, of course. Fair's fair.

—If you don't I'll—

—You'll scream. I know. I won't look. Promise.

She doubted him but she had no more choice. She made her way around the wall, skirting the moth wings, to the place she calculated as furthest from Pete. She squatted so as to face him, keep some kind of lookout, but far as she could tell in the dark, he kept his word.

Finished, she realized the only paper they'd brought remained buried in Ron's pack. Shuffling over there dripping with pants around ankles was not an option, so with wiping a lost cause, she waited and wiggled as many long seconds as she dared before she tugged up her jeans and underwear and scuttled back to her sleeping bags, feeling that much more unclean.

Yet sleep still would not come. Sue-Min continued watching Pete though she saw little more than his blurred dim form. Of all the people to be stuck with in this insane situation. Of course, she'd seen him enough to know that he *was* decent looking, in a corn fed white guy kind of way. Sort of guy who was destined for a career in sales if he didn't become a fireman or a cop. Sandy blond buzz cut, bulked out biceps. He'd go to fat once he had a family, but he didn't and hadn't yet. Stamina would be his best quality in bed. This was a guy who could do pushups for an hour. If only he weren't such a creeper. Yuck.

She shuddered to shake off that train of thought and marshaled her mental focus back to priorities. They might both die here. How long could they survive? They had, she guessed, half a water bottle each plus maybe a backup liter stowed. She knew she did, was pretty sure about Ron. A handful of Clif bars stashed in their packs, possibly some other food too. Her pack held a little Ziploc of walnut halves, another of carrot sticks. That was all. She was pretty sure Pete packed some jerky, and Ron had maybe brought a couple foil-wrapped single serving vacuum packs of salmon or tuna that should still be in his pack. And the worse than useless popcorn. Even if they could make a fire. . . She shuddered at the thought of those tiny explosions in their deliberate silence.

If they stayed trapped for long, water would be their problem before food. She'd noted several fuzzy streaks of algae along the back wall that meant slow trickling seeps, imagined taking turns with Pete licking dirty water from the wall, each of them fighting not to gag or puke. Could she even do it? Could Pete? How thirsty would they have to be first? And would the seeps be enough? No water pooled below them, so the flow could only be agonizing slow.

Pete interrupted her speculations —I'm thinkin' if this thing outside isn't gone in half an hour, I'm goin' out anyway, gonna try to sneak past it, over it, under it, whatever. She saw the faint illumination of the glowstick brush his face. —I don't think it's even. . .

He broke off and slid to his knees then drooped as if deflating till his forehead touched the pebbly floor, groaning a low pained groan all the way down. Sue-Min rose and stepped toward him, closed the gap by near half, but went no closer. He might be feigning only to fool her —Pete? Pete, are you all right?

He took a long time to respond, groaning again before he half-rose and spoke. —My watch. Please tell me it's fucked up. It only says 9:15. It's been way more than three minutes since I checked it. What the hell? What's going on?

—Either way shouldn't the sun be up?

—That's what I mean. We should have sun but we don't. It's like time is speedin' up and slowin' down.

—Now you're talking crazy.

—Am I? Then *you* explain this shit. First it's four in the morning, then all of a sudden it's *nine*. Then half an hour, maybe an hour passes, but it's only three minutes on my watch. What's causin' that? That thing might be weavin' a *web* out of time . . . or maybe it just inhabits some kind of *time vortex* it found, and it sits like an ant lion in its pit, waitin' for its next victim. Which tonight just happens to be us. Or this morning, whichever it really is. . .

—The sun's got to come up sometime. I mean, we *are* in a cave, in a canyon. It's going to take a while longer here, that's all. Don't you think the sky looks lighter outside now? I think it does, a little. Most likely your watch is screwed up. Maybe you bumped it climbing up here.

—I didn't bump it. And it was workin' fine before.

—Well whatever. Maybe these rocks have a high magnetic content, maybe they're messing with your watch. I've heard of caves in El Malpais like that, where a compass doesn't work. Whatever it is, there has to be a natural explanation.

—Oh yeah? *Does that thing outside have a natural explanation?*

—Maybe. Maybe we just don't know the explanation yet.

—Bull-*shit!* That *thing* is a demon or an alien or something from another dimension. There's nothing rational or natural about it!

—Come on Pete. I'm scared as you are, but we've got to keep it together. Talking about demons isn't doing either of us any good. We should be talking about how we're going to get out of here.

—Okay, fine. Hey Sue-*Min*, do you know how we're gonna get out of here?

—I still think your idea of waiting till sunrise was a good one.

—Except maybe there isn't going to *be* any sunrise. Not for us.

—*There has to be.* It's just late because of our location, the canyon, the cave. . .

Pete rested hunched now, haunches on calves, knuckles of his clenched fists jammed down amidst the pebbles.

—What if the sun *never* rises? What if we're caught in this monster's vortex forever?

—What if we wait just a little longer and see if the sun comes up and the monster goes away? Isn't that worth waiting for, when we can walk right out of here, maybe even find Ron? It was your idea anyway.

Pete just shook his head and groaned some more. For several reasons she was trying to keep up a tough front but his apparent collapse wasn't helping. Not one bit. The truth was his comments had begun to get to her, especially his forecast of unending darkness. Shivering, she hugged herself, hoped he didn't see.

Sue-Min told herself Pete's watch was just bumped or broken. It might even start spinning backward next—and if it did, would it take them back to when Ron was still with them? Or were the movements of its damaged hands altogether meaningless, irrelevant to their current situation, the malfunction simply coincidence?

Pete rocked in place, spoke a cryptic sentence —*I say to myself that the earth is extinguished, though I never saw it lit.*

Sue-Min shivered. —What the hell was that about?

He turned to her. —It's from this play I was in, back in my UNM days. Beckett. I have this jones you know, for nerdy smart girls, and one I dated for a while was a theater major. She had this idea I'd be a good actor, kept pushing me to try out for plays she was producing. I finally did and got a part in this Beckett thing. It was weird shit—I played this guy in a wheelchair who kept a bloody handkerchief over his face most of the time. I still remember most of my lines though. My memory's good like that.

Sue-Min struggled to wrap her thoughts around the image of Pete the thespian but it was too much for her to process.

Her mind was already overloaded and all she really wanted to do was go back to sleep, return to the sleeping bag whose upper half still smelled like Ron. Was this faint and fading fragrance all she had left, all that remained? She could not accept that. Ron was resilient, Ron was Ron. Unless she saw definite evidence of his death, she would keep holding out hope he was still alive. And probably needing their help if he was. . .

At home if Sue-Min couldn't get to sleep she would just . . . it was the only thing that helped her fall asleep most nights. How long could she go without jilling off? She thought of the Seinfeld episode, *The Contest*. Hadn't Elaine been the first one out in that?

Pete would want to do the same of course. Would he even make an effort to be discreet? *Ick*. She groaned softly to herself. Once again their situation added levels of complexity to simple quotidian acts.

She shook her head again to clear it then asked Pete — What does your watch say now? She spoke without turning in his direction.

He did not answer immediately, did not turn toward her, did not even look at his watch. Sue-Min kept her peace. It was not as if she had anywhere to go right at the moment.

Finally Pete examined his watch as she observed him. She remembered the device as an old school analog, an inheritance she guessed, his dad's or his granddad's originally. He stared a long minute at the face beneath the crystal but neither moved nor spoke. Finally he said to her without turning —Still 9:15. The second hand moves but I don't think the other hands have even budged from where they were before.

—That's weird.

—You're tellin' me.

His voice was bitter, hopeless, beyond even cynicism. Sue-Min considered how much worse the betrayal of his watch would hurt him if it really were an heirloom. She turned away from him toward the opening and. . .

—Pete! Look! Look outside!

He turned slowly but once he faced the exit she knew he saw what she saw too. The sky *was* lighter now, what she could see of it to either side of the silent immensity at least. No question. The shape of the thing did not resolve itself in relief and continued to defy her efforts to make sense of it overall.

—Do you see it? The sky is definitely getting brighter.

—But that thing is still there.

—Still here *now*. . . We don't know how it got here. We don't know how or when it might leave.

—*If* it leaves. How do we know it's not here to stay?

—Can you be a little less pessimistic? It was your idea anyway about it leaving with the light. Don't you want to test out that thought, see if you were right?

—I don't want to know if I was *wrong*. I just want to get out of here. We've got to find a way to escape.

—Let's see how bright it gets and what the monster does. Come on—if it's really after 9:00 now, we should definitely be getting sunlight down here, even if it's not direct.

It wasn't quite sunlight, but something was changing in the sky, a dim glow visible to either side of the enormous entity. It was an unusual brightness, neither the indigo of twilight nor the poet's rosy fingered dawn. Nor the sun's normal clean yellow-white. Something *was* wrong with this light. Something was *off*. She couldn't even put a color to what was more so just less of the dark than any presence of actual light, and offered no direction of origin as far as she could tell. The central bulk that bore the blossom thing grew no clearer, even in contrast at its sides. The blossom itself grew no less bright.

She glanced at Pete again but he remained concentrated on his watch, his left wrist held close to his face, just below the green tube in his right. Without turning away from it he spoke —You really should come see this, Sue.

—I'll pass.

—Seriously. The hands are all running backwards now. Come see.

Sue-Min didn't like the sound of that but she was no way going to get close enough to see for herself. She was just going to have to trust him about the watch. She was pretty sure she could grant him that, at least from a distance. Even if what he said were true what the hell did it mean for them? She could see the sickly glimmer from outside spreading into the cave like a thin liquid spill, but it signified nothing to her yet.

Sue-Min watched the slow growing glow and Pete watched his watch. The monster remained shapeless, motionless. She glanced at Pete and back and the monster was gone. Fast as that. She missed whether it sank into the canyon or ascended into space. Or blinked out suddenly, faded away slow. . . No sound marked its departure, no flash of light. No wind. Shouldn't some kind of sonic boom have erupted as air rushed into the space it left empty?

Pete remained fixated on his watch. She called to him, a little louder than she would've dared before.

—Pete. Pete, look!

He looked. Paused.

—What happened? Is it doing something?

—I think it's *gone*. It was sudden. It just . . . blinked out. Well, I *blinked* and *it* was gone.

Pete scrambled toward her. She felt a fresh rush of adrenalin but held her ground. What could she do if he really came at her? She should've already grabbed the knife from her pack for protection, or even better the Glock from Ron's. Too late.

He passed her without a glance though, arrived at the entrance. From the dripline Pete looked every direction. —You're right. Holy shit. It's gone. Almost like we dreamed it up.

He stood and hurled the glowstick into the void. Its arc quickly dropped it from her sight, but she saw Pete's chin dip as he followed it down.

—Nothing. It's really gone.

He turned to Sue-Min. —Are you ready to get outta here? For all we know it might come back. We should make time while we can.

Sue-Min was not so sure they should leave the relative safety of the cave. If such a colossus could vanish with neither warning nor coda, how easily could it reappear, catch them in the open? Perhaps that was its plan.

Yet Pete already had his headlamp on and was over the lip, on his way down. —*C'mon! Let's go!*

She wanted to shout —Wait, call for some discussion of options, seek some consensus, but Pete was on the move and hadn't given her any chance for talk. And he had the keys to the truck.

She scrambled to the edge, hung over and called to him. —*Wait!* Give me a minute! I at least have to put my boots on.

Already twice her length below he looked up, nodded, said merely —Hurry!

—What about our packs?

—*Leave the packs.* We've got to move fast, travel light, get back to the truck as quick as we can. We can pick up our packs when we come back with the cops or whoever. Nobody's going to touch our stuff here meantime.

She grabbed her own light from where she'd left it by her pack—safe to use it now she guessed, hoped—began lacing her boots, restrapped her bra. Pete was right. Her pack would only overbalance her on the way back down. They had a window of safety and they'd have to hurry through while it stayed open. However briefly it did. They had no way to tell how long that might be.

When she hunched over the edge she found Pete waiting in the same spot below. His presence gave her comfort, a surprise in itself. Her hands dug for purchase among the dusty pebbles but her feet found good holds, and soon she was below the rim, her hands on solid stone, heading for Pete. He didn't move. As she made her way toward him, he offered encouragement —C'mon, yeah, that's it. Right this way. His steady voice provided a beacon without her looking down.

Soon she was right above him, and for a moment she feared he might grab her ankle and yank her right off the slope, the last witness to whatever he'd gone and done to Ron. That spasm of terror passed and a fresh impulse seized her,

83

the desire to kick Pete right in the face, send *him* tumbling into the slot below. He would never bother her again if she did. Never bother *anyone*. But the keys. . . How badly broken might his body wind up, wedged in the crack below? Would the keys be accessible? What if they flipped from his pocket into the pitch filthy water? She'd never find them, shuddered at the thought of having to reach into that cold opaque foulness, grope blind amongst the sticks and bones. Even if she made it back to the truck without the keys, what could she do? She had no real idea how to hotwire a vehicle. Seek help from the ranchers? Hike out all the way on her own? What if the police found her bootprint pressed onto Pete's forehead?

The moment passed. She could not do it. She was no murderer. Her Baptist upbringing on the farm held that far.

Pete continued his descent and she followed. Though she had to feel with her feet for footholds, she found her handholds on the ribbed rock face with relative ease, and descended keeping just above Pete. They shared no more words till they arrived right above the coffee colored creek at the bottom of the crack, where Pete had to comment —Phase One done at least. And we're making good time I think . . . not that I can tell anymore. . . Now we've gotta get up and outta here. Are you ready?

—Yeah.

She was scanning ahead and behind for any remnant of Ron's broken body, but she saw nothing in her little headlamp's limited beam beyond the stony V, the stagnant water, the scattered broken ends of branches or bones. No Ron. And still no monster.

Pete began to chimney along the crack back the way they'd come, and two seconds later she followed. He didn't look back.

As Sue-Min rushed to keep up her left hand slipped and her foot sunk half up her calf in the stagnant ink. Right off she felt the cold and cried out, an exclamation half gasp half yelp. She stopped her fall with her forearm, her submerged foot finding no bottom, and wriggled to brace herself anew, but before she could yank her wet foot free, Pete was there to take her arm, offer support. She would've shooed him off but her scraped palm already throbbed and the water was cold and who knew what worse?

—C'mon, he said, —Grab my arm, and she paused only a moment before wrapping first her right hand then her left around his bicep. She could feel the damage to her hand— after everything, she'd forgotten her gloves *again. Damn.* Pete raised her till her boot rose dripping from the black wet and held her in place until she could get her hands back against the sides of the crevice higher up. She shook her foot back and forth, for what little good it did. The water had run down inside her boot.

—You okay? Did you hurt yourself?

—Just wet. And angry at myself for slipping.

—Not your fault. It's dark and we're both rushing. Maybe I was rushing too much. Sorry. It must feel gross.

—Don't make me think about it.

—Yeah. Understood. Let's keep going then. I want to get up and out of this canyon as quick as we can. If that thing comes back, I figure it will show up here, and I want to be far away by then.

He led on and she followed, taking extra care now to maintain three points of contact with the walls at all times, grimacing each time she moved her left foot and felt her sodden wool sock squish inside her boot.

The limited beam from Sue-Min's weak LED light fell mainly on Pete's advancing back, the khaki shirt he wore a broad reflective canvas. As she watched his halting forward motion she considered the exchange they just shared, the way he helped her. He'd been civil, gentlemanly, even compassionate. The same guy who tried to force himself on her only a couple hours ago. Maybe being afraid a monster would eat him brought out the best in his personality. If only a giant monster were chasing him every minute in his life, he might become a decent guy, maybe even pick up where he left off on his theater career, learn to tap dance, acquire an interest in show tunes. . .

She almost laughed at her thoughts but caught the laugh in her throat so only a strangled hiccup emerged.

Pete didn't stop or turn around but asked —What was that? You okay? You need a break?

—No, I'm fine. Let's keep going.

Soon they reached a spot Pete identified as where they'd come down before, though it all looked the same to her in the dark. How hard would it be to retrace their route if they didn't come up in the right place?

But Pete was asking if she was ready, and why argue? They began their ascent, which was shorter and easier than their descent and did not take long.

Once at the top they followed the cliff edge back, scanning for landmarks in what terrain their lights revealed, searching for where they'd first come out on the canyon's rim, each suggesting this tree might or might not look familiar, that bush, this twisted snag. They could see only hints of the opposite face, and nothing of the chasm now far below. The odd gray light Sue-Min thought might have been dawn had departed, and the moon had set as well. The stars, though bright now, offered very little illumination.

Neither of them spoke about it aloud, but she was certain Pete shared her fear they had come up *past* the point they were seeking, and were now wandering further up Blossom Creek Canyon than they'd been so far—and if they were, how long would it be before they figured it out? They might go a mile if the canyon ran that long before it boxed off.

When Pete at last claimed they'd arrived at that spot where they first reached the cliff, Sue-Min was sure he was wrong. She would recall *that* outcrop, *that* juniper leaning out over the void. She didn't argue though. What good would it do? Following Pete was easy enough. If he were wrong, they'd still find their way in time, though they might have to double back. With her own volition exhausted, allowing Pete to lead was the simple option. Let him get the credit or take the blame if they got lost. She wanted nothing but to get out of the canyon, get in the truck, get help. They progressed into the wood. She stopped trying to decide whether she'd come this way before.

They picked their way between outcrops and trees, leafless branches showing stark in their headlamps against the black background. Sue-Min began to consider just *how* lost they could get out here. But they had to hit the Blue River eventually, didn't they?

—Whoa! Pete stopped cold, spoke in his stage whisper again, left hand splayed out behind his back as if to hold her back. —You see that?

—See what? And then she did. A pale pink gleam backlit the trees ahead, shining the same hue as the blobs that wandered through the cave.

She took the two strides that brought her up beside Pete and halted, but she couldn't see any better from there, just the trees silhouetted against a strange stretch of pale rosy light. —What is it?

—Damned if I know. I thought it might be the dawn for a sec, but no, it's wrong.

—Is it that *thing?* What if all we did was walk right up to its lair?

—I don't think so. The color isn't right, and the light starts at the ground. That thing would have to be lying down. Let's get a little closer.

Together they picked their way to the edge of a clearing, saw ahead sheets of diffuse pink light rising from the ground—no, not the ground itself but from rows of stones. It was the same place they'd puzzled over the strange linear alignments of rocks. A cold light rose now from the rocks— no, not the rocks themselves so much as from the patterns they formed on the ground, as if these arcs and arms marked the foundations of translucent walls rising into the sky, not fading overhead so much as growing hard to follow from the angle of their height. Sue-Min wondered how the effect would look from the high above.

She spoke softly —No way am I going near there. Not after those things hit me in the cave.

—You said they didn't hurt you, that you didn't feel anything.

—I said I didn't feel *much* but I didn't feel nothing either. I don't even want to think about what the aftereffects might be. I don't want to think about *anything* right now, Pete. I just want to get the hell out of here.

—Yeah. Damn. Well I agree. Let's not go close to that light. At least we know we're on the right track though—we definitely came by those stones on the way out. Now I'm kind of sorry we walked through them even then—if that's some kind of radiation they're giving off they might've been doing it before only we couldn't see it because of the sun was too bright.

They skirted the open patch to what Sue-Min thought was the south, all but dodging from tree to tree and keeping a watch on the curving rosy walls as if the light might somehow notice them. The light did nothing but ascend and glow—it neither dimmed nor shimmered nor brightened nor moved. It showed no sign it recognized their presence, but they were glad to get well around it nonetheless.

As Pete said, at least they knew where they were. Sort of. They had passed the stones before, come right across them. Their path *had* come this way. Now if they could pick up its thread from here and follow it back.

Pete led the way until at last they came to the edge of a ridge. Sue-Min was sure they were somewhere near the spot from where she'd last glimpsed the truck the day before. Pete agreed. —Let's hope our luck holds out.

Their *luck* . . . the word struck Sue-Min as absurd in this context. How could anyone see this experience as *lucky?*

What prize had Ron won? Nothing held the same meaning anymore. Words had become as unreliable as Pete's watch.

They began following the ridge down. Though they could see nothing of the abyss to their left, and only the barest outlines of the mountains in the west, they were sure the hidden valley of the Blue lay below. They made good time down, the only mishap when Sue-Min stumbled once and fell against a trunk, scraping her hurt hand even worse. Again Pete came to her aid but this time she waved him off.

They reached the valley floor. They crossed the meager Blue. They did not find the truck. Pete cursed and kicked the ground, held his arms out, spun around. —It was right here. I'm sure! Those fucking rednecks! They took it!

Sue-Min shone her fading light on the ground. —I don't see any tracks. There should be tracks if the truck was here. The ground is damp enough from the river we're leaving tracks right now. See? She stepped with her left, lifted her foot, pointed at the shallow imprint of her boot sole fixed in her beam.

Pete stepped toward her, saw, turned to view the path of his own passage. —What the. . . ?

Sue-Min meanwhile spun a slow circle, and around 260 degrees caught a gleam as of chrome or glass. She saw it through the shadows of the shut gate. They were inside the gate and on the ranch. —Pete, look, *there*. She pointed. He turned and directed his light at the gate. Did he see the truck parked beyond? Was that what she had seen?

She twisted around again at a sound, a sort of grunt or huff behind her. Something rustled in the brush. She could not see much, but was that the golden glint of an eye in the night?

—Pete, I think a bull is behind us.

He looked back, and though he didn't say what he saw, he spoke softly but firmly —Run for the gate. And he ran.

Sue-Min ran too, hit the gate and grappled up its aluminum struts, always expecting a horn to pierce her kidney, her buttock, her thigh, toss her to the ground where she could be trampled and gored. Two strands of barbed wire ran across the top of the gate, the gap only a few inches. —Here, said Pete beside her, and lifted the bottom wire with a gloved hand between two barbs. —Go!

She levered up sideways, hugging the top rail, and slipped beneath the wire. Her feet hit the ground and she took two steps before she remembered Pete, rushed back to the gate and returned the favor.

It would've sucked to come all this way just to get killed by a bull. But they were over the gate, and no bull had rushed them. Now they'd be safe once they got in the truck. They'd escaped the monster, they'd escaped the bull. All they needed now was to escape the Blue.

The truck stood where they parked it. Intact.

Pete looked at her —I was sure those ranchers did something with it. After what Ron said in the cave. I thought it would be gone, I really did.

—It looks okay. She walked around to the passenger side. Tires and windows all good. No visible damage.

—Yeahhh. Then —Let's get outta here.

—You've still got the keys, right?

—Hell yeah I do! He drew the keys from his right pants pocket and unlocked the driver's side door. He started the truck first then unlocked her door from the inside. Chivalry was dead for him once again. Sue-Min found this return to form almost reassuring after the out of character manners and kindness he'd shown twice during their escape.

The moment she joined him and had the door shut, even before she had her belt on, he swung them in a backwards curve toward the signs, then straightened the wheel and they were on their way out.

—Made it, Pete said. —Thank God!

Sue-Min had heard many examples of people lost or trapped and rescued only by the alleged *grace of God*. Those who called it that ignored all the people who didn't survive. What had God done for those folks? Were they denied his grace? What had God done for Ron? How was Pete more deserving than Ron? How was she?

They rode in silence at first, Pete navigating the twists and bumps, obviously going as fast as he dared in the darkness. After more than a minute he turned to her and said —Wanna see something really scary?

—Seriously? Are you fucking kidding?

—Yeah, I was kidding. It's a line from a movie. I guess you haven't seen it. Oh well, your loss. You would've laughed if you got it.

Half a silent minute passed, then —How about a joke?

She had no will to argue. —Sure. Whatever.

—Okay, so it's the Old West, on a train from Houston to El Paso. This beautiful woman is riding unescorted on the train, and they're barely out of the station before an obvious

New Yorker turns to her and asks her if she'll get it on with him between cars for two dollars. The woman hides her blushing face behind her fan and says loudly —Will no man here defend a woman's honor?

About two seconds later this Texan gets up and without a word draws and shoots the Yankee right through the heart, then sits down again like it was nothing. The lady says — Thank you sir, for defending my honor.

—Honor, hell, the old cowboy says, and spits tobacco. —I'm not letting any Easterner come out here and raise the price of women in Texas.

Sue-Min stared ahead at the emptiness beyond their headlights while the truck jounced over ruts in the ungraded road. She took a series of long deep breaths. But she couldn't hold it in.

—That's your idea of a joke, Pete? That super-sexist bullshit? That's the kind of stuff you think is funny?

—Aw, c'mon, lighten up. That's a classic! And it's not against women—it's anti-Texan. Everyone in New Mexico likes to make fun of Texans. It's a *tradition!*

—Just when I began to think you might have a decent side, you remind me what an asshole you are. Are you trying to make *sure* I report you when we get to a police station?

Right off she recognized her mistake. They were still in Pete's truck, still in a remote area. He could do just about anything. She began to estimate how far a lead she could get on foot if she jumped out and ran when he stopped the truck.

—I didn't try to rape you! I flirted with you and you turned me down. End of story. Nothing wrong with that, except maybe your loss.

—I didn't *turn you down!* I threatened to yell loud enough the monster outside would hear! She imagined explaining this in her testimony, in a police station, in a courtroom. How much of her story was monster-dependent? Sue-Min clenched her fists, choked down her response, looked straight ahead. And without a thought she began to scream, pounding the dashboard with bloody palms as she allowed it all to pour out in a long wordless cry sectioned only by her necessary breath. Ron, the rape attempt, the monster . . . she howled it all out.

—Stop it! Pete shouted, —Stop it stop it stop it! You've *got* to lighten up! In her peripheral vision she saw him shake his head side to side, though he did not slow the truck.

She stopped screaming, though not because of Pete. She finally felt done.

—Look, I just want to get out of here, get to a police station, tell them Ron is missing, get a rescue op started. Anything else . . . it can wait. So please just drive, and no more jokes, okay?

—Sure, sure. Not like you've got a sense of humor anyway.

He paused then added —You really think there's a chance Ron is still alive out there?

—I don't know. If he's not we need to find his body at least. The image came to her unbidden—Ron's broken body, jammed into the crack, face submerged in the foul dark water.

—We don't know what happened to him. He might still be alive.

—True, I suppose, but what do you think the police will say if we talk about weird lights and monsters? We need to get our stories straight before—

The truck lurched suddenly, wheels rumbling against the undercarriage. Pete wrestled with the wheel.

—What the hell was that?

—I don't know! It was like the road shifted underneath us or something. Probably we went through some mud or sand or—

The ground buckled beneath them and lifted the whole truck suddenly upward. Metal crumpled, wheels spun in air and Sue-Min felt that sick too-fast elevator feeling—then the vast shimmering petals spread across the great dark bulk below and her stomach dropped out altogether. For a moment before they tumbled in they saw what opened at the center of the bloom. Then they lost all sight.

*Thank you for picking up this King Shot Press title. We are a small press based in Portland, Oregon, dedicated to the publication of fine works of prose and poetry. If you loved reading the book you hold in your hands, do please tell your friends about it. For more information about us, see www.kingshotpress.com.*

**Also Available from King Shot Press**

*Leverage* by Eric Nelson
*Strategies Against Nature* by Cody Goodfellow
*Killer &Victim* by Chris Lambert
*Marigold* by Troy James Weaver
*I Miss The World* by Violet LeVoit